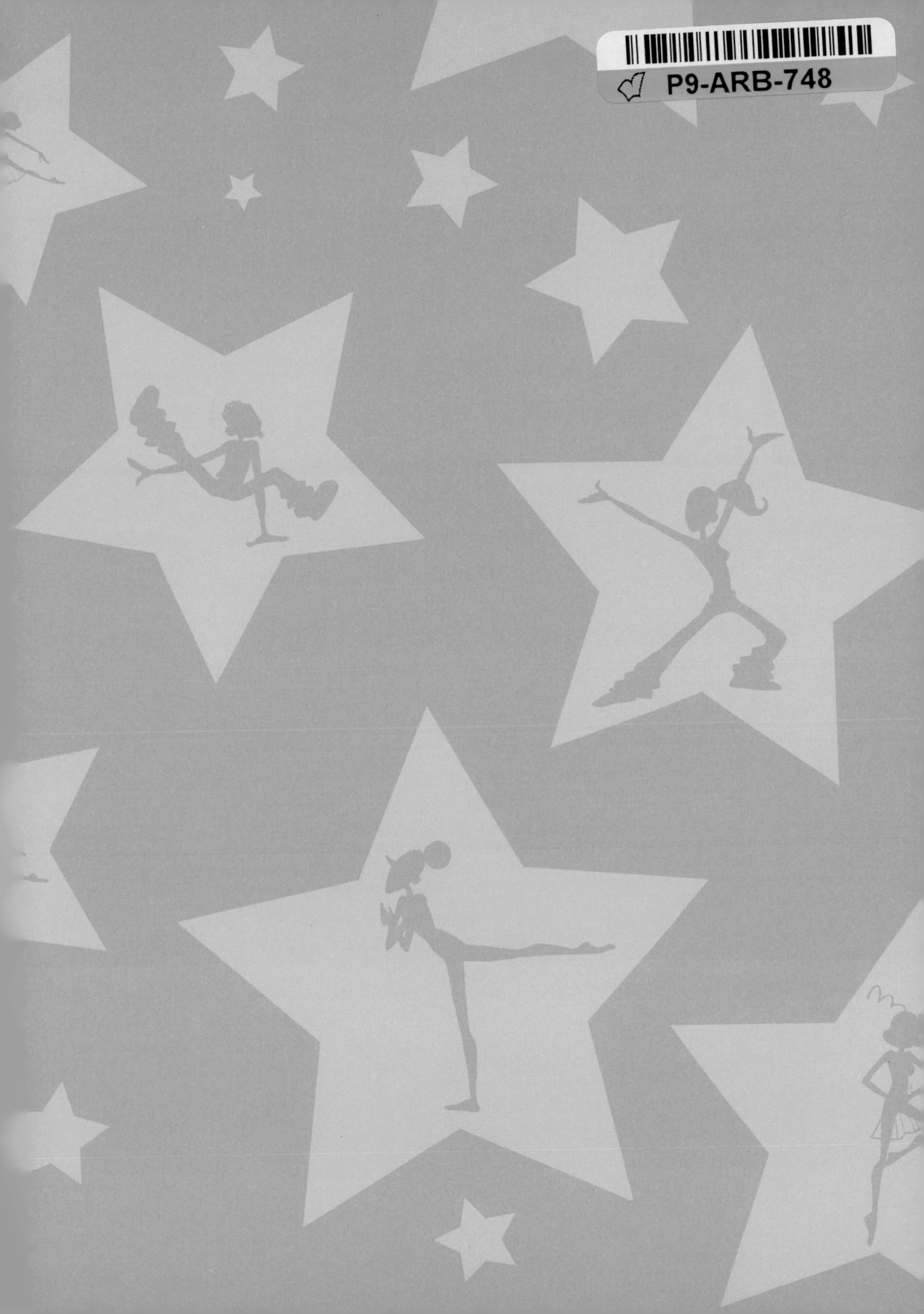

Dance Class

Béka • Writer

Crip • Artist

Maëla Cosson • Colorist

PAPERCUTZ™

New York

Dance Class Graphic Novels available from PAPERCUTZ™

Béka and Crip
Dance Class
So, You Think You Can Hip-Hop?
PAPERCUTZ

#1 "So, You Think You Can Hip-Hop?"

Béka and Crip
Dance Class
Romeos and Juliet
PAPERCUTZ

#2 "Romeos and Juliet"

Béka and Crip
Dance Class
African Folk Dance Fever
PAPERCUTZ

#3 "African Folk Dance Fever"

Dance Class

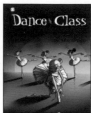

#4 "A Funny Thing Happened on the Way to Paris..."

Béka and Crip
Dance Class
To Russia, With Love
PAPERCUTZ

#5 "To Russia, With Love"

Béka and Crip
Dance Class
A Merry Olde Christmas
PAPERCUTZ

#6 "A Merry Olde Christmas"

Béka and Crip
Dance Class
PAPERCUTZ

#7 "School Night Fever"

Béka and Crip
Dance Class
Snow White and the Seven Dwarves
PAPERCUTZ

#8 "Snow White and the Seven Dwarves"

Béka and Crip
Dance Class
Dancing in the Rain
PAPERCUTZ

#9 "Dancing in the Rain"

Béka and Crip
Dance Class
Letting It Go
PAPERCUTZ

#10 "Letting It Go"

Béka and Crip
Dance Class
Dance with Me
PAPERCUTZ

#11 "Dance with Me"

Dance Class
The New Girl

#12 "The New Girl"

Béka and Crip
3 Graphic Novels in 1
Dance Class
3 in 1
PAPERCUTZ

DANCE CLASS 3 IN 1 #1

Béka and Crip
3 Graphic Novels in 1
Dance Class
3 in 1
PAPERCUTZ

DANCE CLASS 3 IN 1 #2

Béka and Crip
3 Graphic Novels in 1
Dance Class
3 in 1
PAPERCUTZ

DANCE CLASS 3 IN 1 #3

Béka and Crip
3 Graphic Novels in 1
Dance Class
3 in 1
PAPERCUTZ

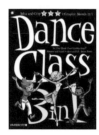

DANCE CLASS 3 IN 1 #4 COMING SOON!

SEE MORE AT PAPERCUTZ.COM • Also available digitally wherever e-books are sold.

Dance Class

DANCE CLASS #12
"The New Girl"
BÉKA — Writer
CRIP — Artist
MAËLA COSSON — Colorist
MARK McNABB — Production
JOE JOHNSON — Translation
WILSON RAMOS JR. — Lettering
JORDAN HILLMAN — Editorial Intern
JEFF WHITMAN — Managing Editor
JIM SALICRUP
Editor-in-Chief

Special thanks to
CATHERINE LOISELET

ISBN: 978-1-5458-0883-2

Printed in China
November 2021

Papercutz books may be purchased for busines or promotional use. For information on bulk purchases please contact Macmillan Corporate Premium Sales Department at (800) 221-7945 x5442.

Distributed by Macmillan
First Papercutz Printing

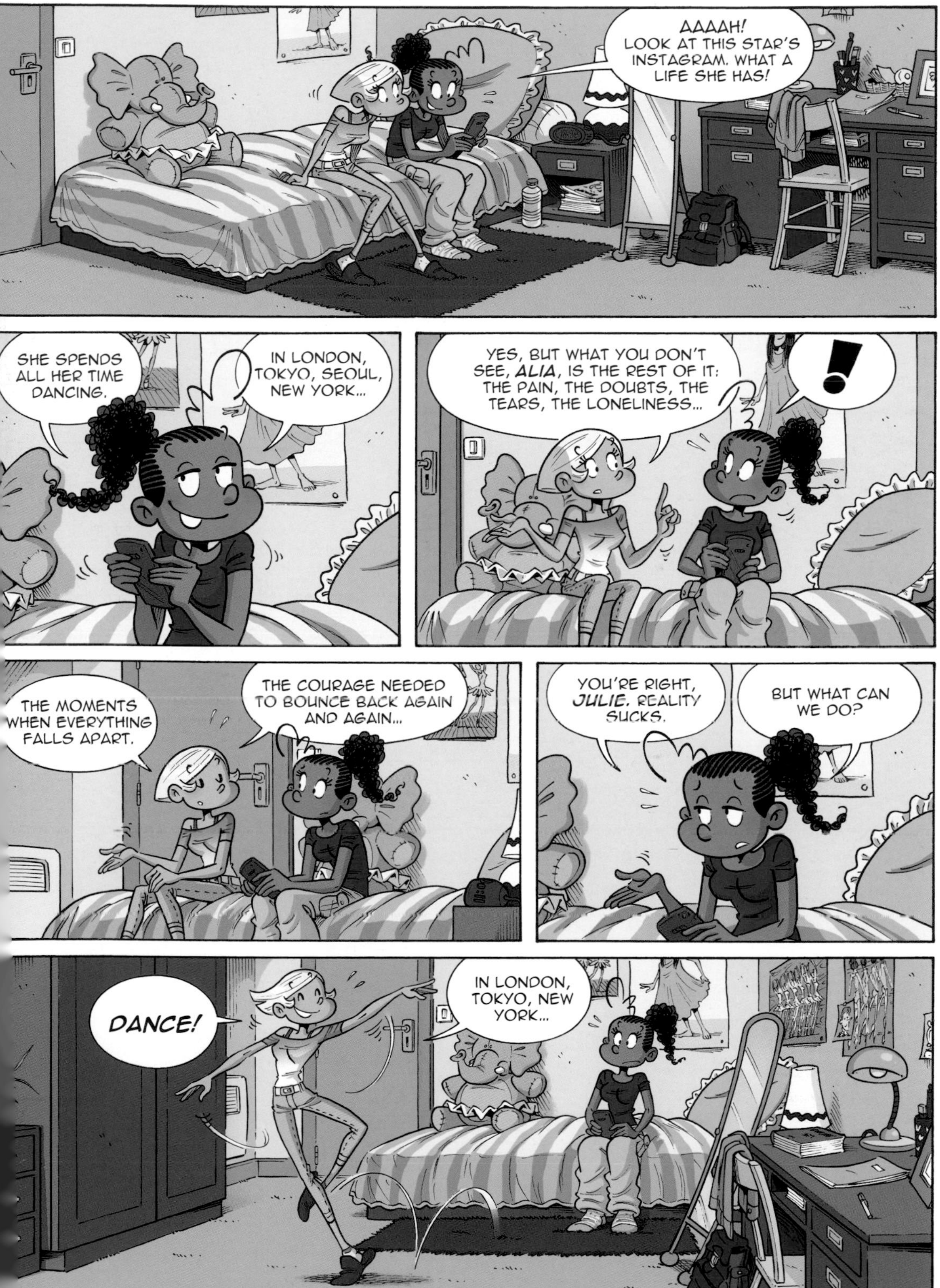

AAAAH! LOOK AT THIS STAR'S INSTAGRAM. WHAT A LIFE SHE HAS!
SHE SPENDS ALL HER TIME DANCING.
IN LONDON, TOKYO, SEOUL, NEW YORK...
YES, BUT WHAT YOU DON'T SEE, ALIA, IS THE REST OF IT: THE PAIN, THE DOUBTS, THE TEARS, THE LONELINESS...
!
THE MOMENTS WHEN EVERYTHING FALLS APART.
THE COURAGE NEEDED TO BOUNCE BACK AGAIN AND AGAIN...
YOU'RE RIGHT, JULIE. REALITY SUCKS.
BUT WHAT CAN WE DO?
DANCE!
IN LONDON, TOKYO, NEW YORK...

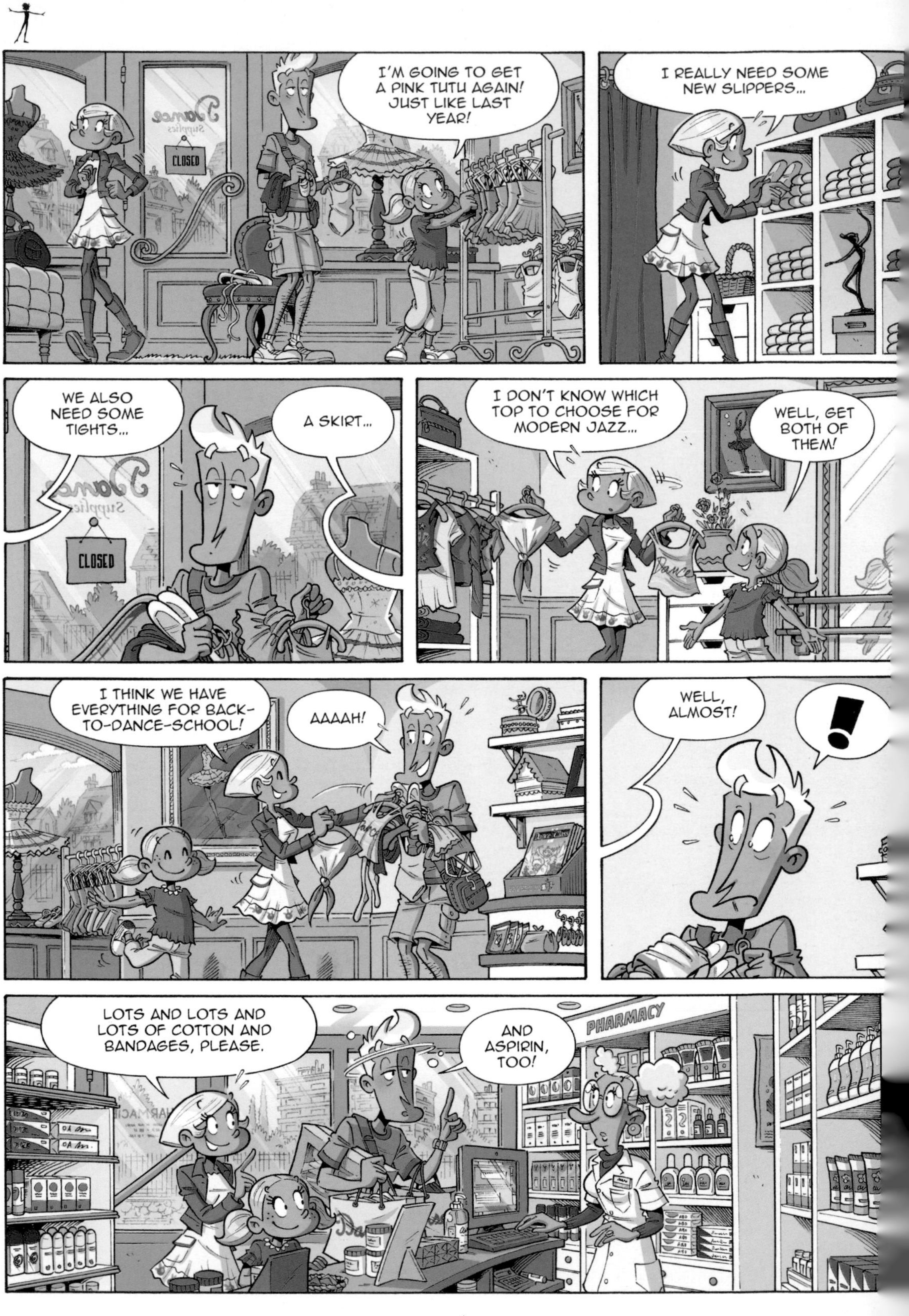
I'M GOING TO GET A PINK TUTU AGAIN! JUST LIKE LAST YEAR!
CLOSED
I REALLY NEED SOME NEW SLIPPERS...
WE ALSO NEED SOME TIGHTS...
A SKIRT...
CLOSED
I DON'T KNOW WHICH TOP TO CHOOSE FOR MODERN JAZZ...
WELL, GET BOTH OF THEM!
I THINK WE HAVE EVERYTHING FOR BACK-TO-DANCE-SCHOOL!
AAAAH!
WELL, ALMOST!
!
LOTS AND LOTS AND LOTS OF COTTON AND BANDAGES, PLEASE.
AND ASPIRIN, TOO!
PHARMACY

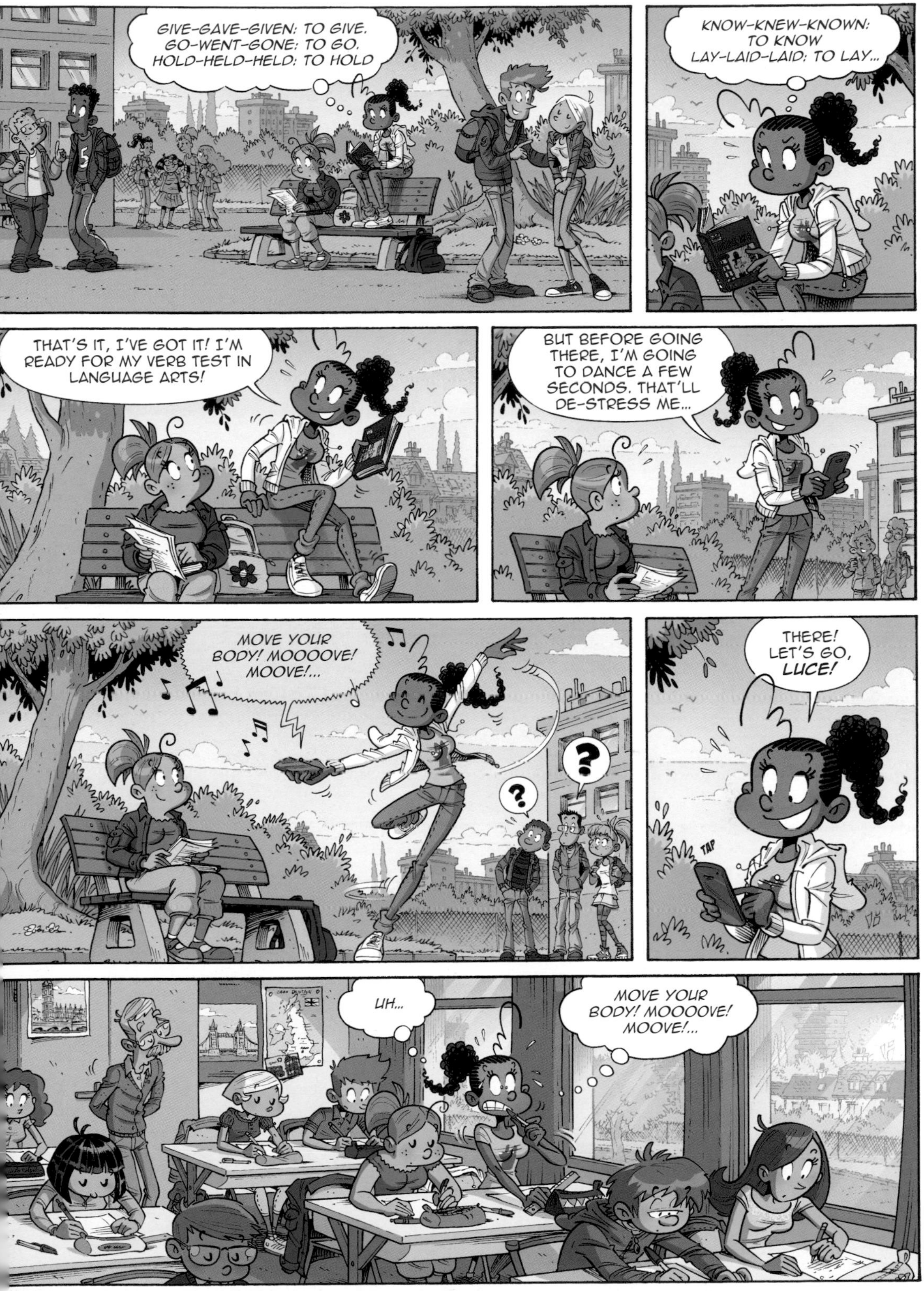
GIVE-GAVE-GIVEN: TO GIVE. GO-WENT-GONE: TO GO. HOLD-HELD-HELD: TO HOLD
KNOW-KNEW-KNOWN: TO KNOW LAY-LAID-LAID: TO LAY...
THAT'S IT, I'VE GOT IT! I'M READY FOR MY VERB TEST IN LANGUAGE ARTS!
BUT BEFORE GOING THERE, I'M GOING TO DANCE A FEW SECONDS. THAT'LL DE-STRESS ME...
MOVE YOUR BODY! MOOOOVE! MOOVE!...
?
?
THERE! LET'S GO, LUCE!
TAP
UH...
MOVE YOUR BODY! MOOOOVE! MOOVE!...

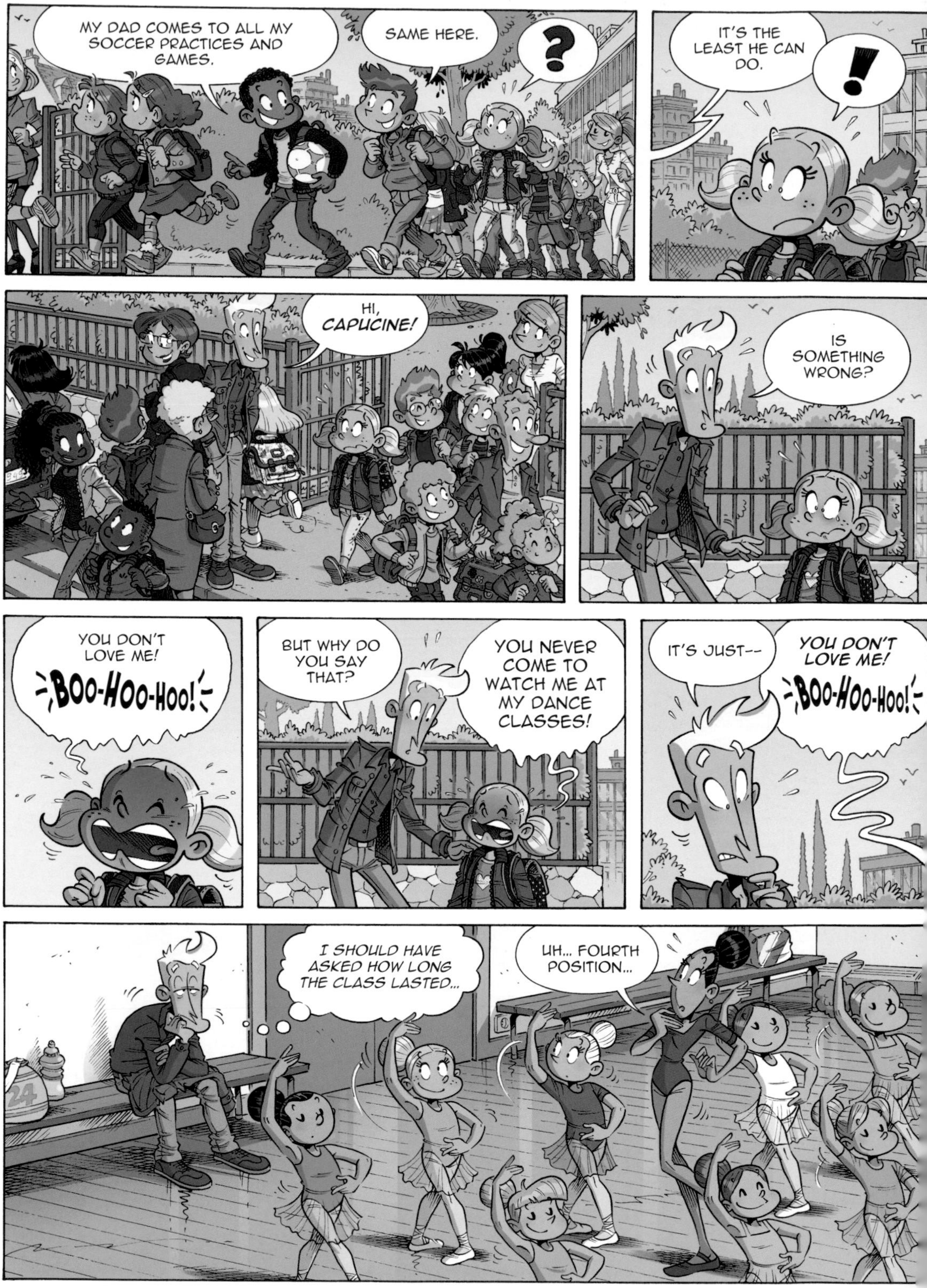
MY DAD COMES TO ALL MY SOCCER PRACTICES AND GAMES.
SAME HERE.
?
IT'S THE LEAST HE CAN DO.
!
HI, CAPUCINE!
IS SOMETHING WRONG?
YOU DON'T LOVE ME!
BOO-HOO-HOO!
BUT WHY DO YOU SAY THAT?
YOU NEVER COME TO WATCH ME AT MY DANCE CLASSES!
IT'S JUST--
YOU DON'T LOVE ME!
BOO-HOO-HOO!
I SHOULD HAVE ASKED HOW LONG THE CLASS LASTED...
UH... FOURTH POSITION...

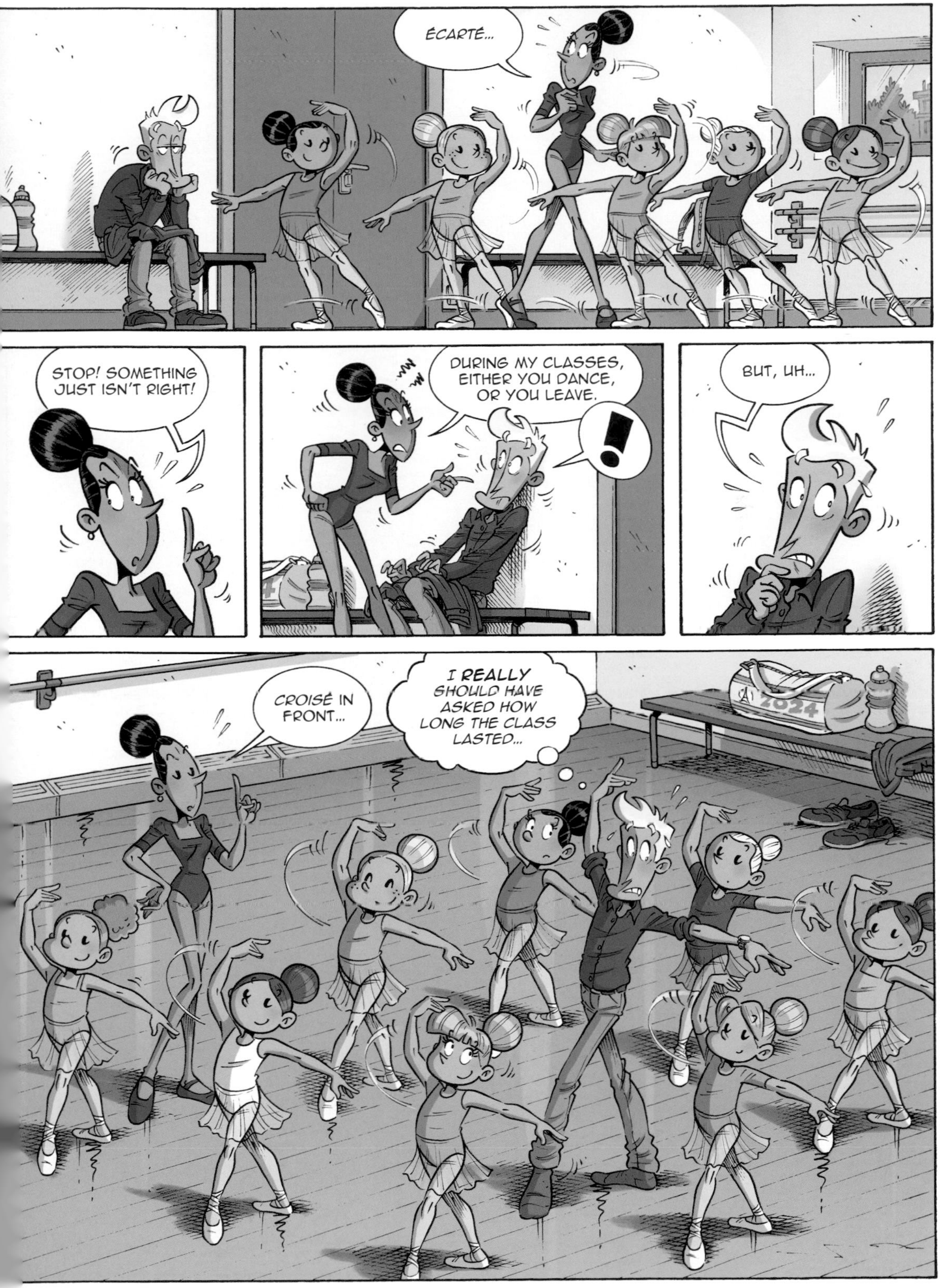
ÉCARTÉ...
STOP! SOMETHING JUST ISN'T RIGHT!
DURING MY CLASSES, EITHER YOU DANCE, OR YOU LEAVE.
!
BUT, UH...
CROISÉ IN FRONT...
I REALLY SHOULD HAVE ASKED HOW LONG THE CLASS LASTED...
2024

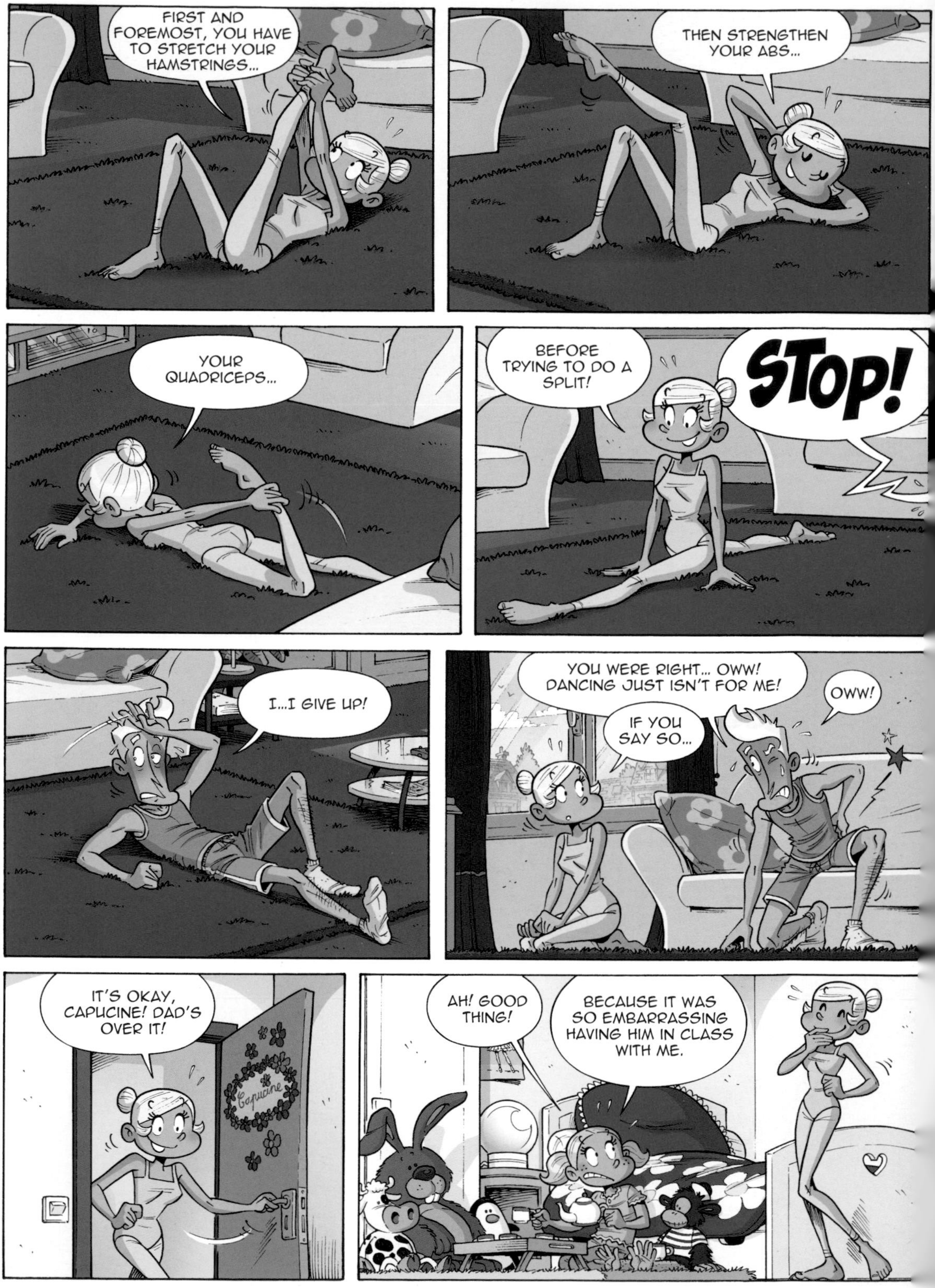

FIRST AND FOREMOST, YOU HAVE TO STRETCH YOUR HAMSTRINGS...
THEN STRENGTHEN YOUR ABS...
YOUR QUADRICEPS...
BEFORE TRYING TO DO A SPLIT!
STOP!
I...I GIVE UP!
YOU WERE RIGHT... OWW! DANCING JUST ISN'T FOR ME!
IF YOU SAY SO...
OWW!
IT'S OKAY, CAPUCINE! DAD'S OVER IT!
Capucine
AH! GOOD THING!
BECAUSE IT WAS SO EMBARRASSING HAVING HIM IN CLASS WITH ME.

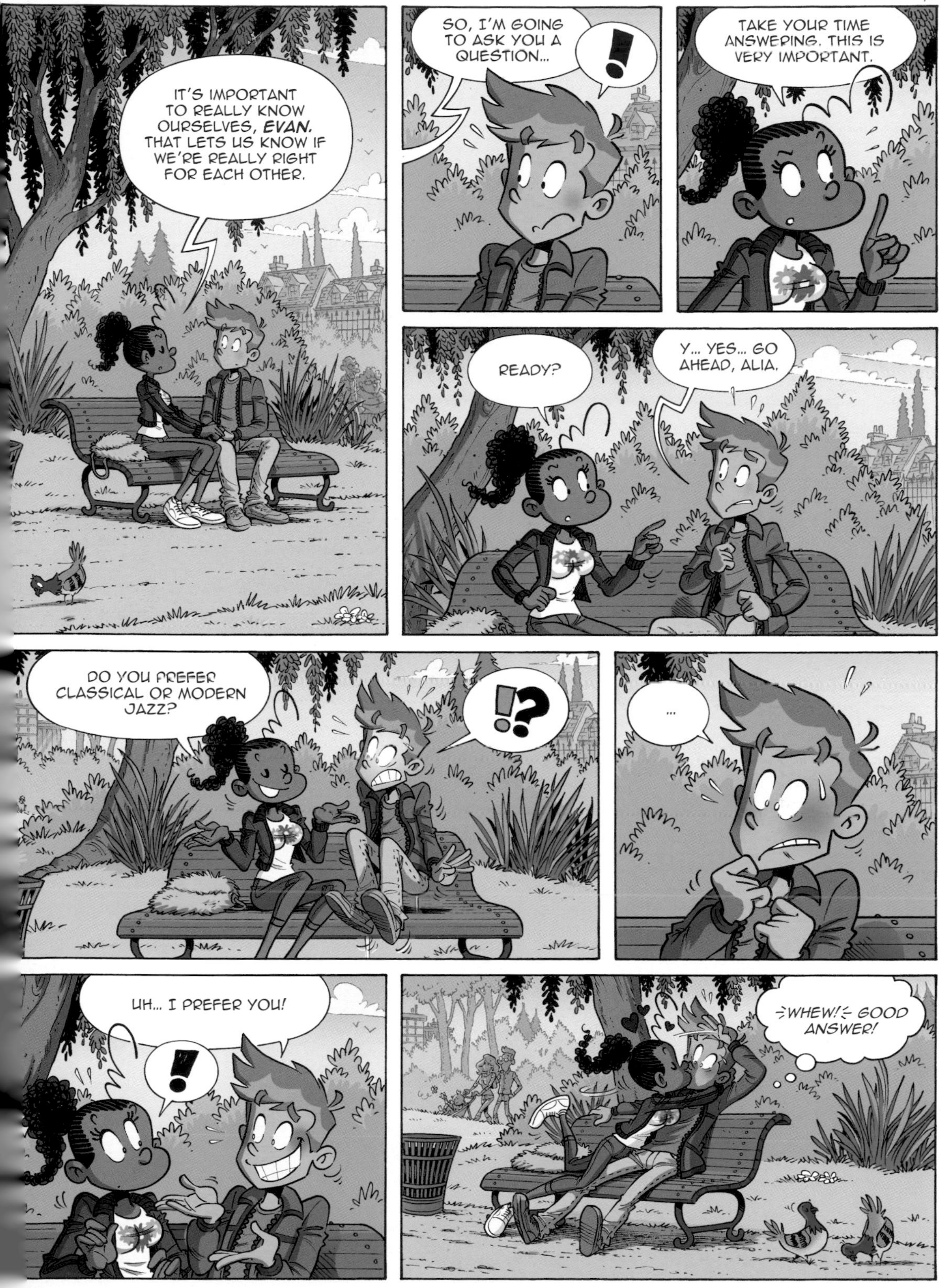
IT'S IMPORTANT TO REALLY KNOW OURSELVES, EVAN. THAT LETS US KNOW IF WE'RE REALLY RIGHT FOR EACH OTHER.
SO, I'M GOING TO ASK YOU A QUESTION...
!
TAKE YOUR TIME ANSWERING. THIS IS VERY IMPORTANT.
READY?
Y... YES... GO AHEAD, ALIA.
DO YOU PREFER CLASSICAL OR MODERN JAZZ?
!?
...
UH... I PREFER YOU!
!
WHEW! GOOD ANSWER!

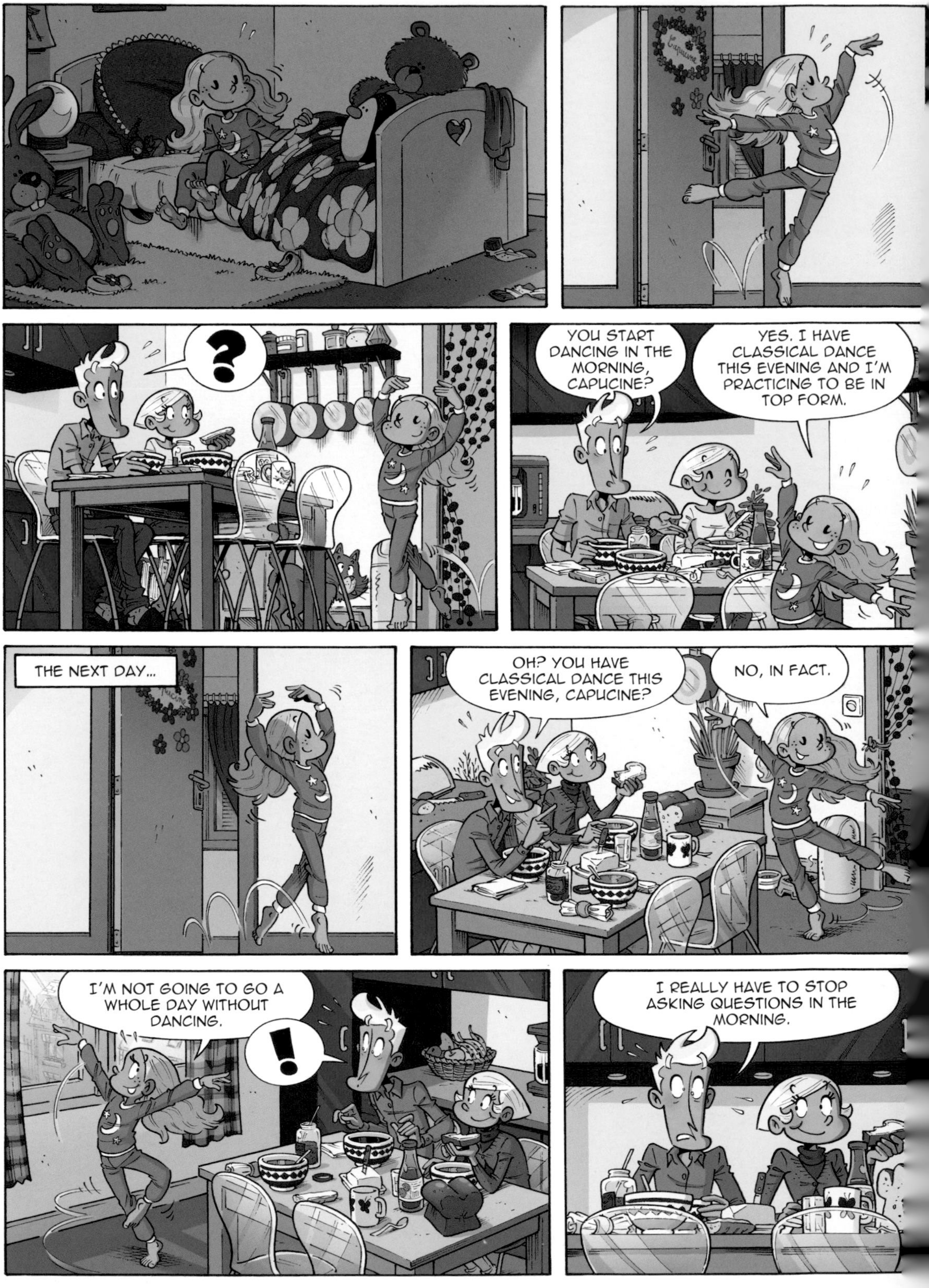
?
YOU START DANCING IN THE MORNING, CAPUCINE?
YES. I HAVE CLASSICAL DANCE THIS EVENING AND I'M PRACTICING TO BE IN TOP FORM.
THE NEXT DAY...
OH? YOU HAVE CLASSICAL DANCE THIS EVENING, CAPUCINE?
NO, IN FACT.
I'M NOT GOING TO GO A WHOLE DAY WITHOUT DANCING.
!
I REALLY HAVE TO STOP ASKING QUESTIONS IN THE MORNING.

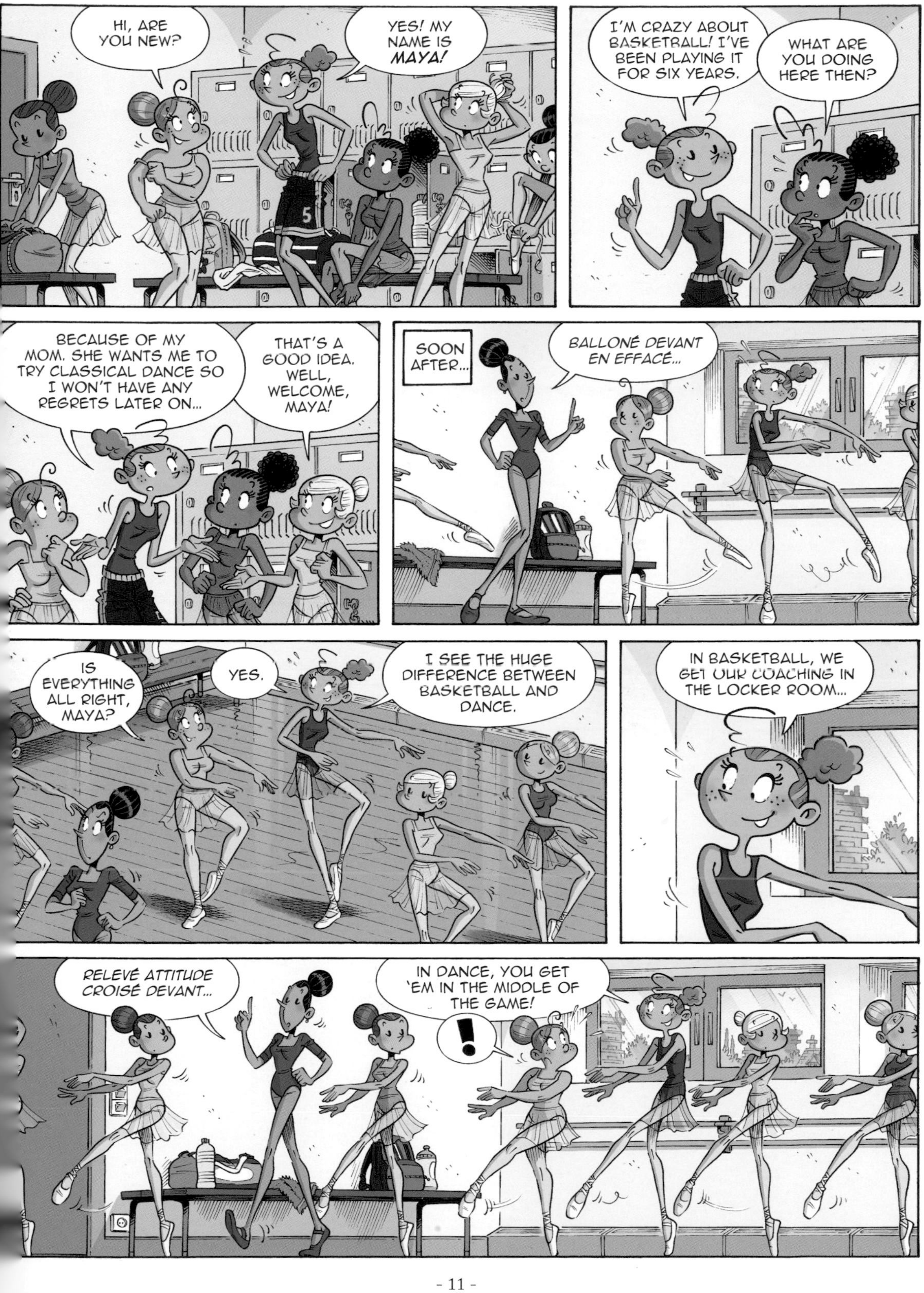
HI, ARE YOU NEW?
YES! MY NAME IS MAYA!
I'M CRAZY ABOUT BASKETBALL! I'VE BEEN PLAYING IT FOR SIX YEARS.
WHAT ARE YOU DOING HERE THEN?
BECAUSE OF MY MOM. SHE WANTS ME TO TRY CLASSICAL DANCE SO I WON'T HAVE ANY REGRETS LATER ON...
THAT'S A GOOD IDEA. WELL, WELCOME, MAYA!
SOON AFTER...
BALLONÉ DEVANT EN EFFACÉ...
IS EVERYTHING ALL RIGHT, MAYA?
YES.
I SEE THE HUGE DIFFERENCE BETWEEN BASKETBALL AND DANCE.
IN BASKETBALL, WE GET OUR COACHING IN THE LOCKER ROOM...
RELEVÉ ATTITUDE CROISÉ DEVANT...
IN DANCE, YOU GET 'EM IN THE MIDDLE OF THE GAME!
!

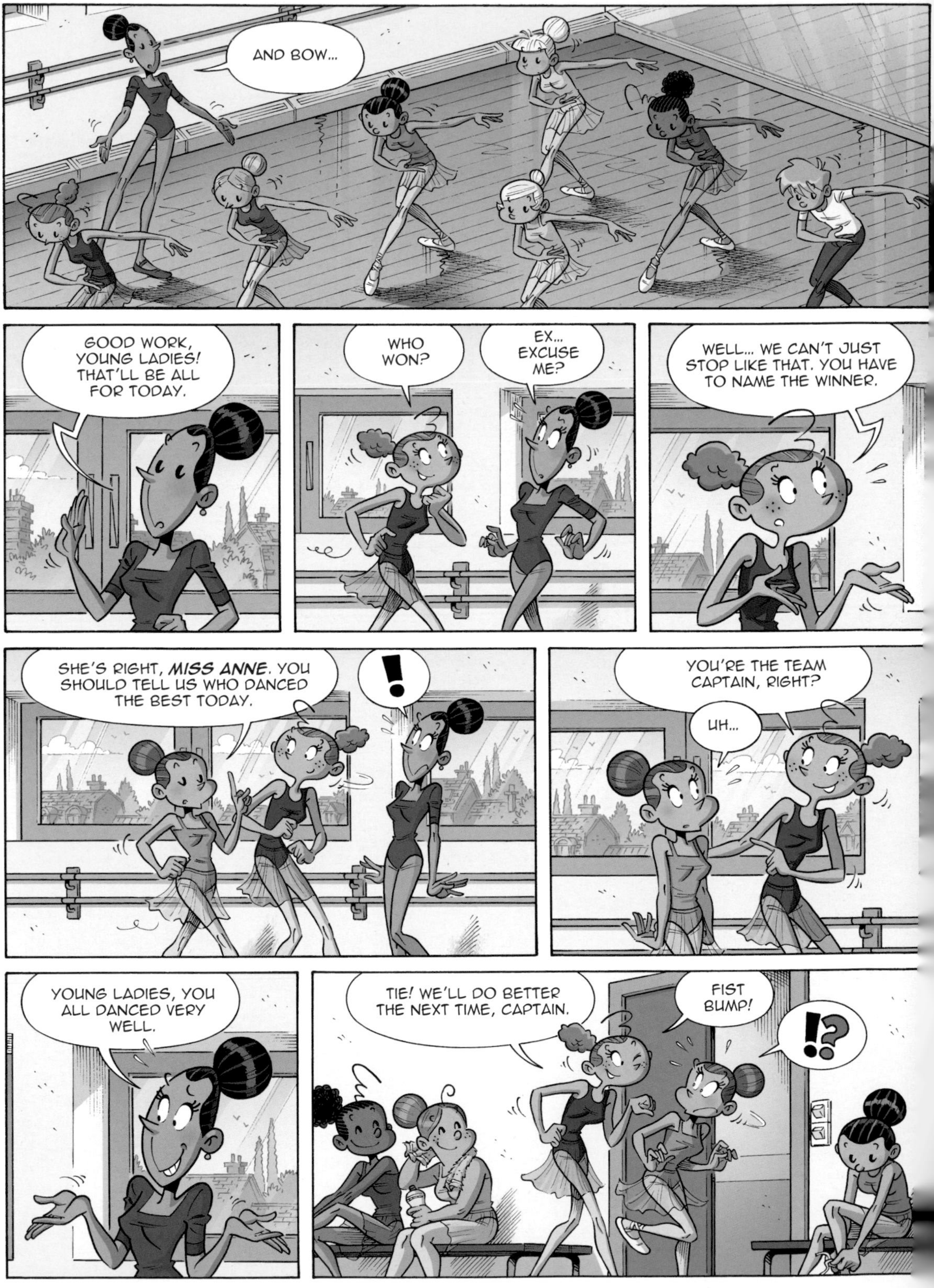
AND BOW...
GOOD WORK, YOUNG LADIES! THAT'LL BE ALL FOR TODAY.
WHO WON?
EX... EXCUSE ME?
WELL... WE CAN'T JUST STOP LIKE THAT. YOU HAVE TO NAME THE WINNER.
SHE'S RIGHT, MISS ANNE. YOU SHOULD TELL US WHO DANCED THE BEST TODAY.
!
YOU'RE THE TEAM CAPTAIN, RIGHT?
UH...
YOUNG LADIES, YOU ALL DANCED VERY WELL.
TIE! WE'LL DO BETTER THE NEXT TIME, CAPTAIN.
FIST BUMP!
!?

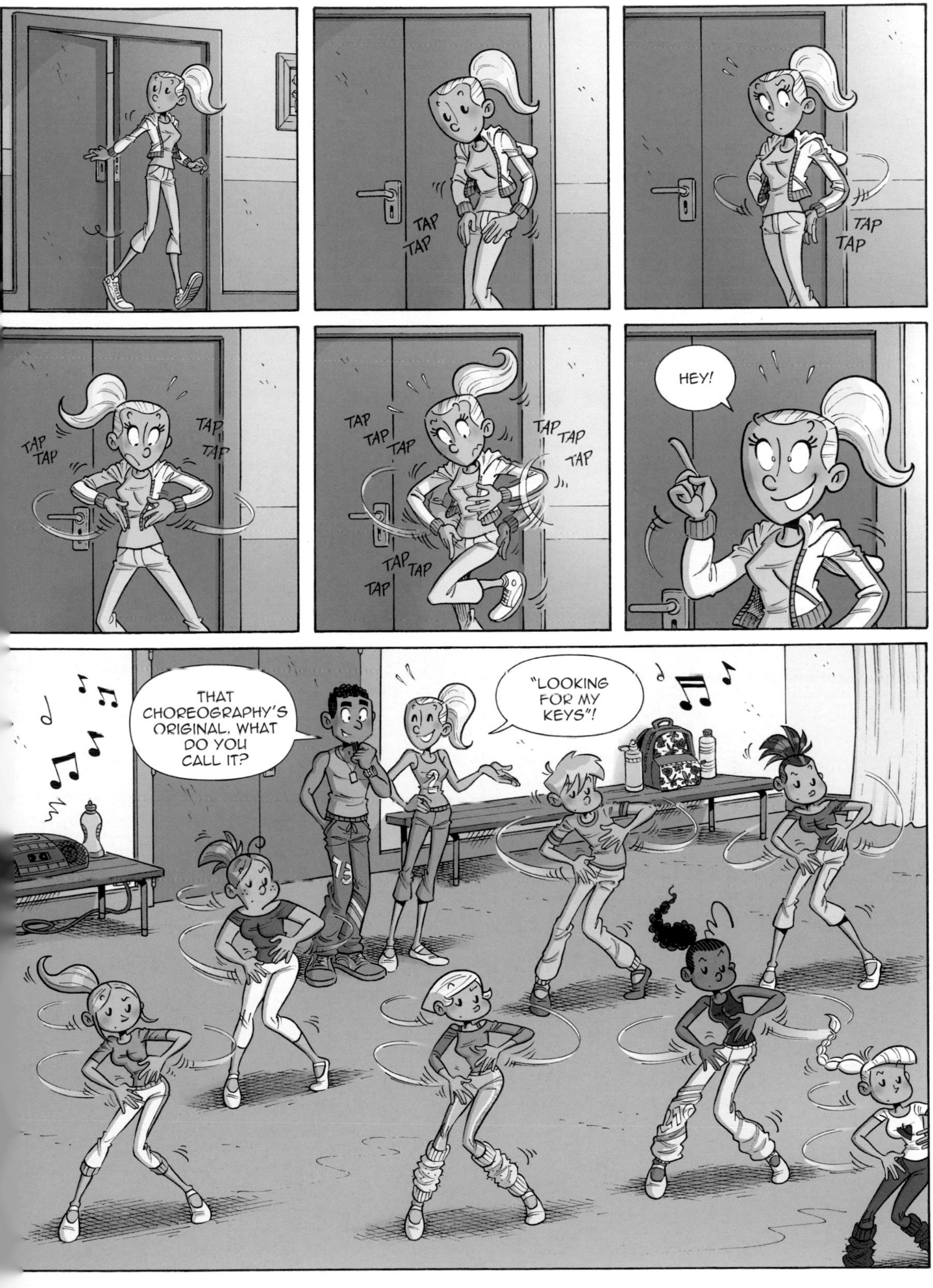
TAP
TAP
TAP
TAP
TAP
TAP
TAP
TAP
TAP
TAP
TAP
TAP
TAP
TAP
TAP
TAP
TAP
HEY!
THAT CHOREOGRAPHY'S ORIGINAL. WHAT DO YOU CALL IT?
"LOOKING FOR MY KEYS"!

BATTEMENT TENDU CROISÉ DERRIÈRE...

COACH!

?

UH... YES, MAYA?

I WAS WONDERING IF OUR OFFENSE WASN'T ATTACKING WITH A BATTEMENT TENDU CROISÉ TOO OFTEN...

WOULDN'T IT BE BETTER TO TRY A BALANCÉ OR A SISSONNE FERMÉ?

THEN, WE'D PIVOT TO A PAS DE CHAT... IT'D THROW OUR OPPONENT OFF!

WHAT DO YOU THINK, COACH?

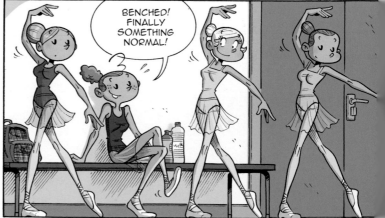

BENCHED! FINALLY SOMETHING NORMAL!

- 14 -

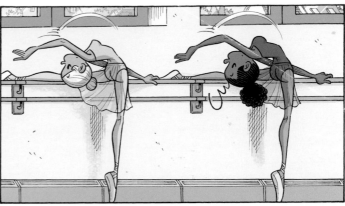

ALL DONE! THAT'LL BE ENOUGH STRETCHING FOR TONIGHT, ALIA.

IF YOU LIKE, WE COULD DO OUR HOMEWORK TOGETHER NOW.

OKAY!

≥PFFFFF!≤

MATH IS ALL GREEK TO ME! IT'S GOT MY HEAD ALL TURNED UPSIDE DOWN.

JOHNNY BONGOS

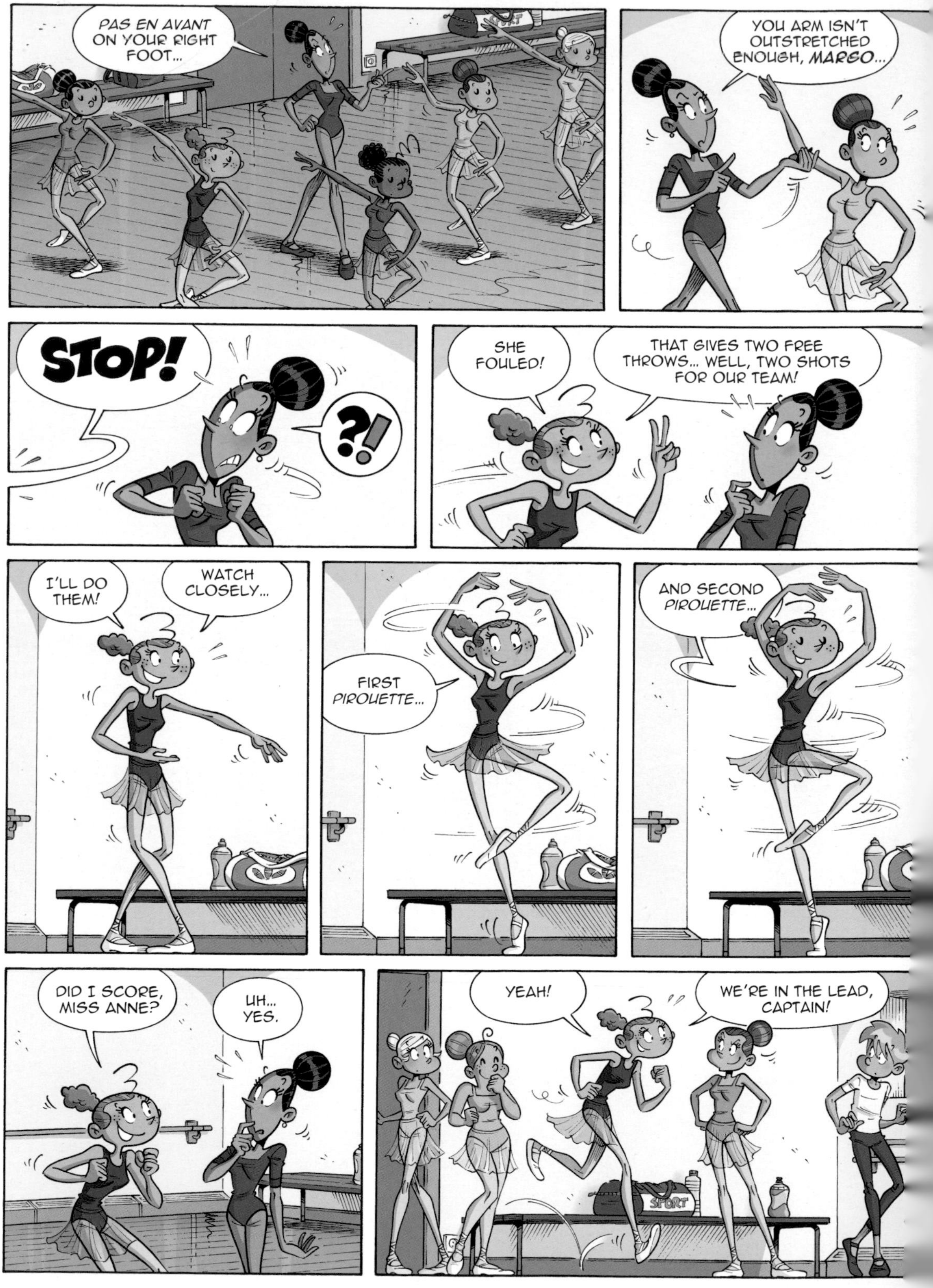
PAS EN AVANT ON YOUR RIGHT FOOT...
SPORT
YOU ARM ISN'T OUTSTRETCHED ENOUGH, MARGO...
STOP!
?!
SHE FOULED!
THAT GIVES TWO FREE THROWS... WELL, TWO SHOTS FOR OUR TEAM!
I'LL DO THEM!
WATCH CLOSELY...
FIRST PIROUETTE...
AND SECOND PIROUETTE...
DID I SCORE, MISS ANNE?
UH... YES.
YEAH!
WE'RE IN THE LEAD, CAPTAIN!
SPORT

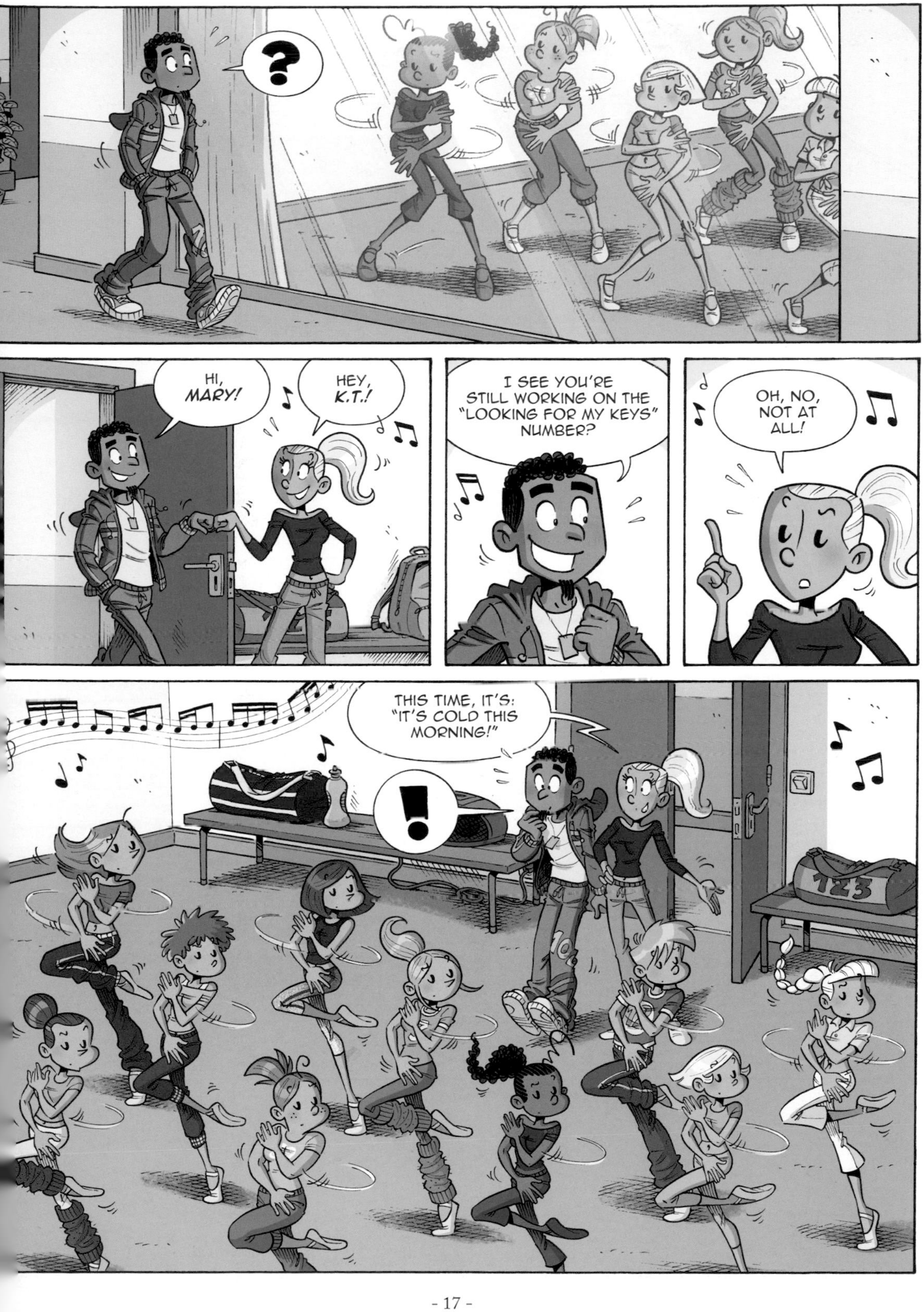
?
HI, MARY!
HEY, K.T.!
I SEE YOU'RE STILL WORKING ON THE "LOOKING FOR MY KEYS" NUMBER?
OH, NO, NOT AT ALL!
THIS TIME, IT'S: "IT'S COLD THIS MORNING!"
!

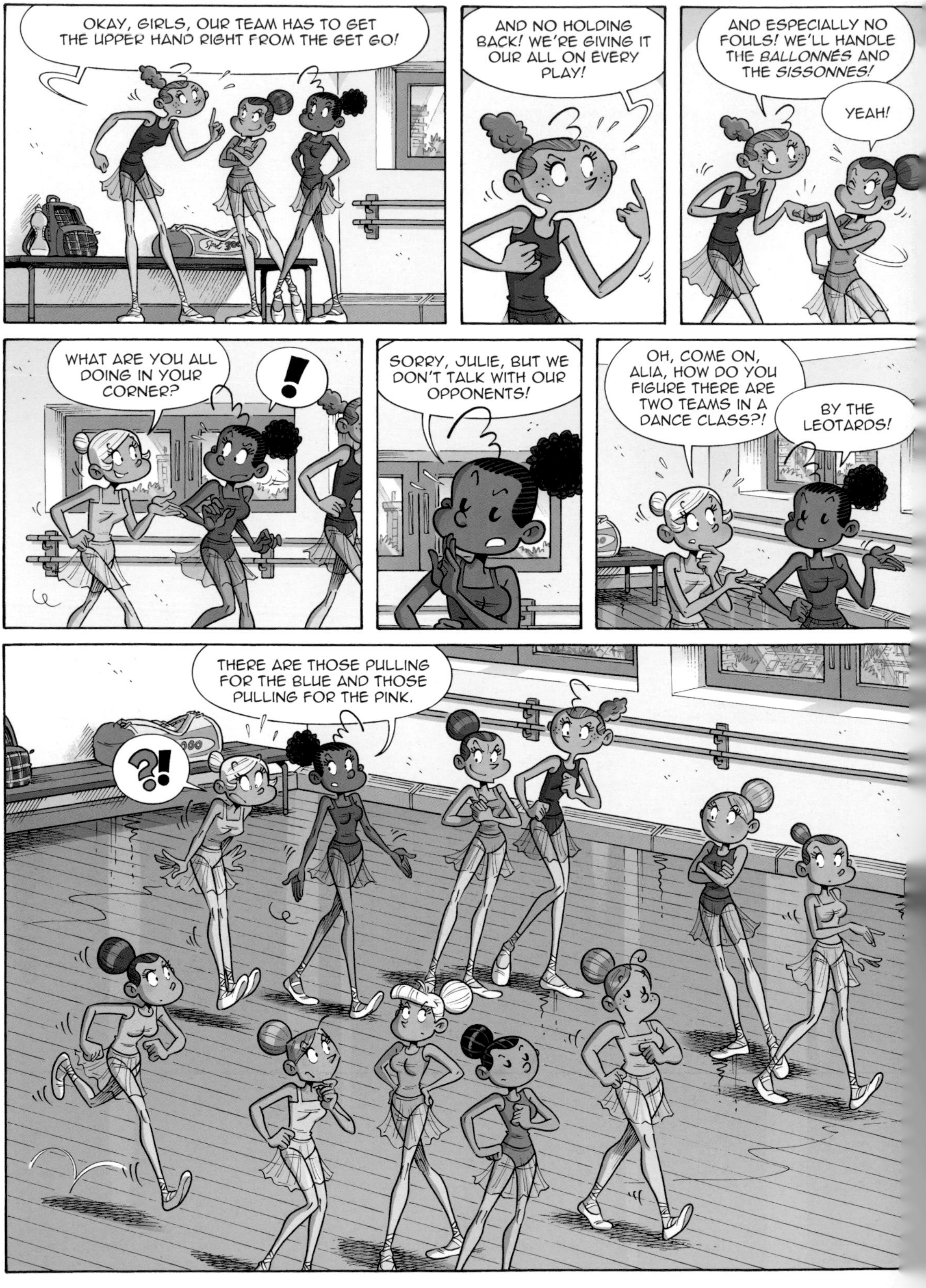
OKAY, GIRLS, OUR TEAM HAS TO GET THE UPPER HAND RIGHT FROM THE GET GO!
AND NO HOLDING BACK! WE'RE GIVING IT OUR ALL ON EVERY PLAY!
AND ESPECIALLY NO FOULS! WE'LL HANDLE THE BALLONNÉS AND THE SISSONNES!
YEAH!
WHAT ARE YOU ALL DOING IN YOUR CORNER?
!
SORRY, JULIE, BUT WE DON'T TALK WITH OUR OPPONENTS!
OH, COME ON, ALIA, HOW DO YOU FIGURE THERE ARE TWO TEAMS IN A DANCE CLASS?!
BY THE LEOTARDS!
THERE ARE THOSE PULLING FOR THE BLUE AND THOSE PULLING FOR THE PINK.
?!

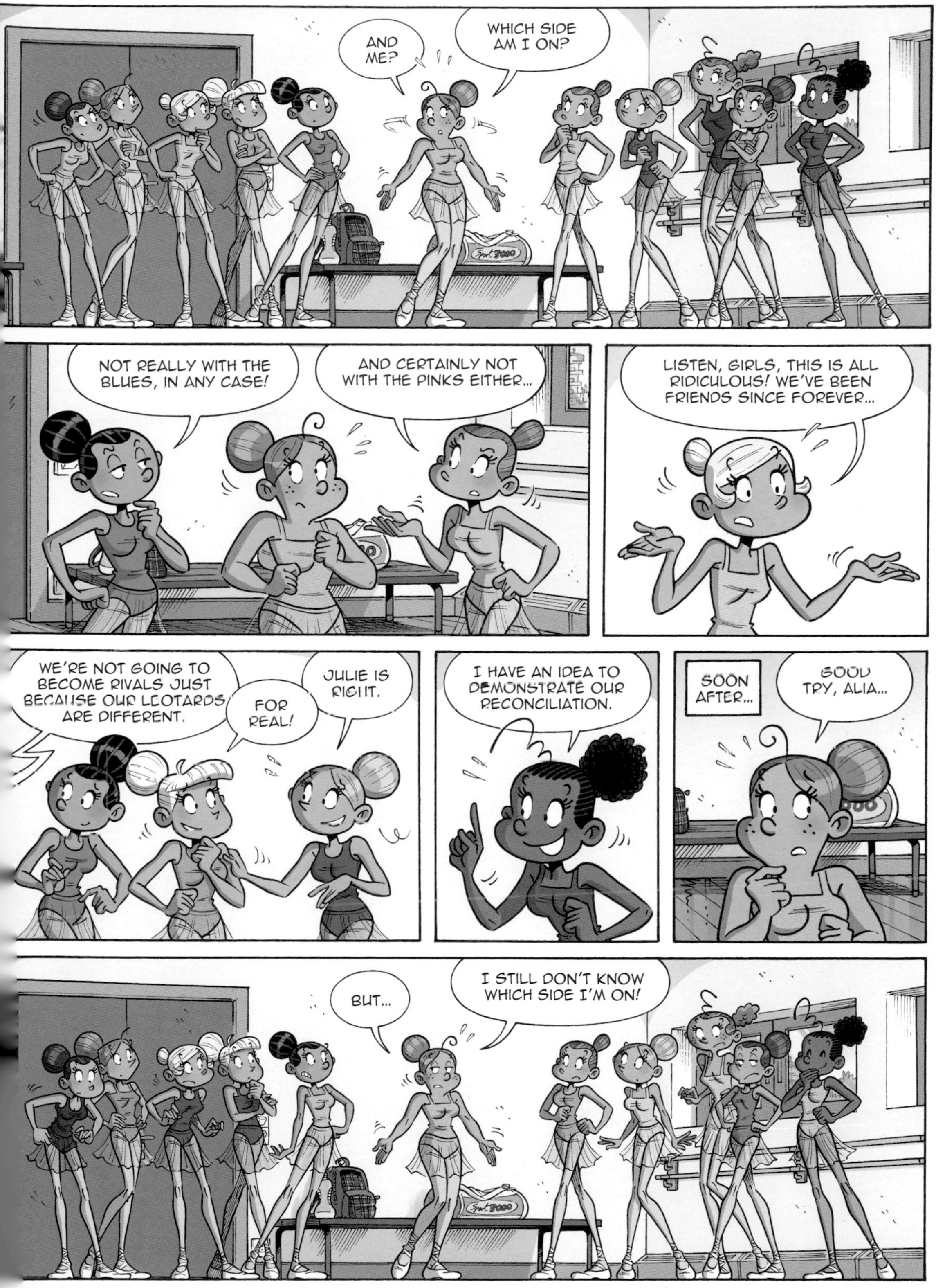

AND ME?
WHICH SIDE AM I ON?
NOT REALLY WITH THE BLUES, IN ANY CASE!
AND CERTAINLY NOT WITH THE PINKS EITHER...
LISTEN, GIRLS, THIS IS ALL RIDICULOUS! WE'VE BEEN FRIENDS SINCE FOREVER...
WE'RE NOT GOING TO BECOME RIVALS JUST BECAUSE OUR LEOTARDS ARE DIFFERENT.
FOR REAL!
JULIE IS RIGHT.
I HAVE AN IDEA TO DEMONSTRATE OUR RECONCILIATION.
SOON AFTER...
GOOD TRY, ALIA...
BUT...
I STILL DON'T KNOW WHICH SIDE I'M ON!

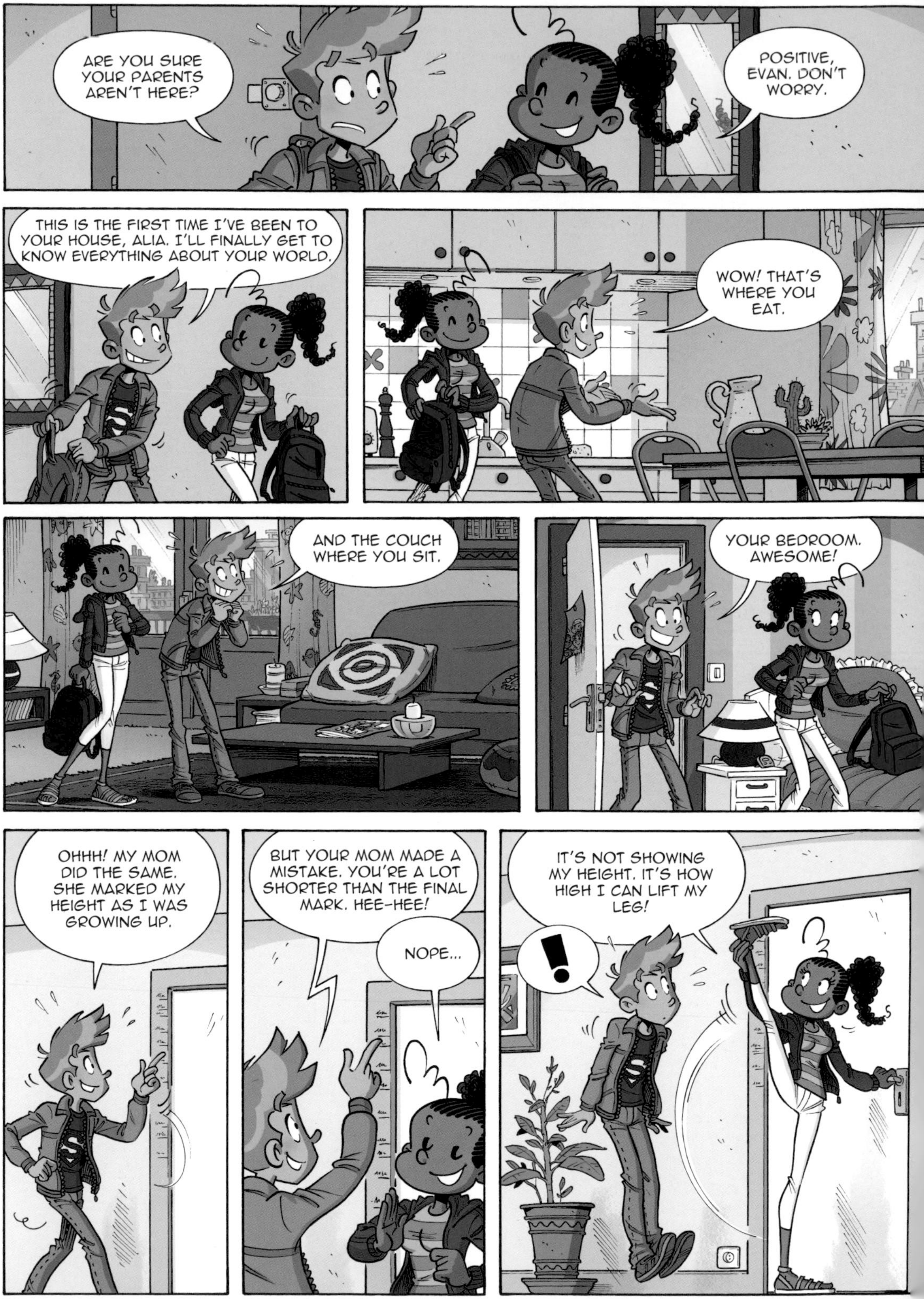
ARE YOU SURE YOUR PARENTS AREN'T HERE?
POSITIVE, EVAN. DON'T WORRY.
THIS IS THE FIRST TIME I'VE BEEN TO YOUR HOUSE, ALIA. I'LL FINALLY GET TO KNOW EVERYTHING ABOUT YOUR WORLD.
WOW! THAT'S WHERE YOU EAT.
AND THE COUCH WHERE YOU SIT.
YOUR BEDROOM. AWESOME!
OHHH! MY MOM DID THE SAME. SHE MARKED MY HEIGHT AS I WAS GROWING UP.
BUT YOUR MOM MADE A MISTAKE. YOU'RE A LOT SHORTER THAN THE FINAL MARK. HEE-HEE!
NOPE...
IT'S NOT SHOWING MY HEIGHT. IT'S HOW HIGH I CAN LIFT MY LEG!
!

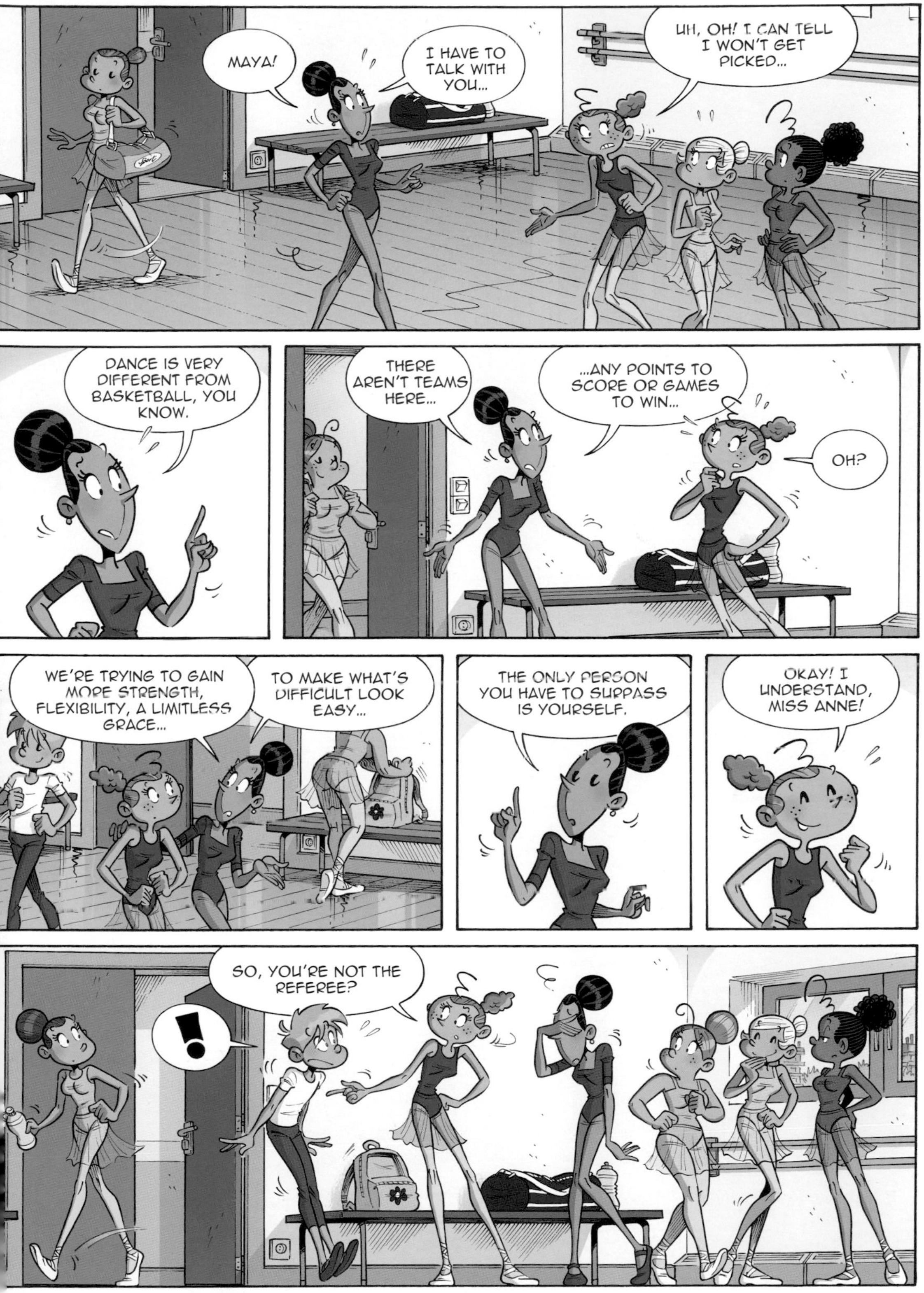
MAYA!
I HAVE TO TALK WITH YOU...
UH, OH! I CAN TELL I WON'T GET PICKED...
DANCE IS VERY DIFFERENT FROM BASKETBALL, YOU KNOW.
THERE AREN'T TEAMS HERE...
...ANY POINTS TO SCORE OR GAMES TO WIN...
OH?
WE'RE TRYING TO GAIN MORE STRENGTH, FLEXIBILITY, A LIMITLESS GRACE...
TO MAKE WHAT'S DIFFICULT LOOK EASY...
THE ONLY PERSON YOU HAVE TO SURPASS IS YOURSELF.
OKAY! I UNDERSTAND, MISS ANNE!
SO, YOU'RE NOT THE REFEREE?
!

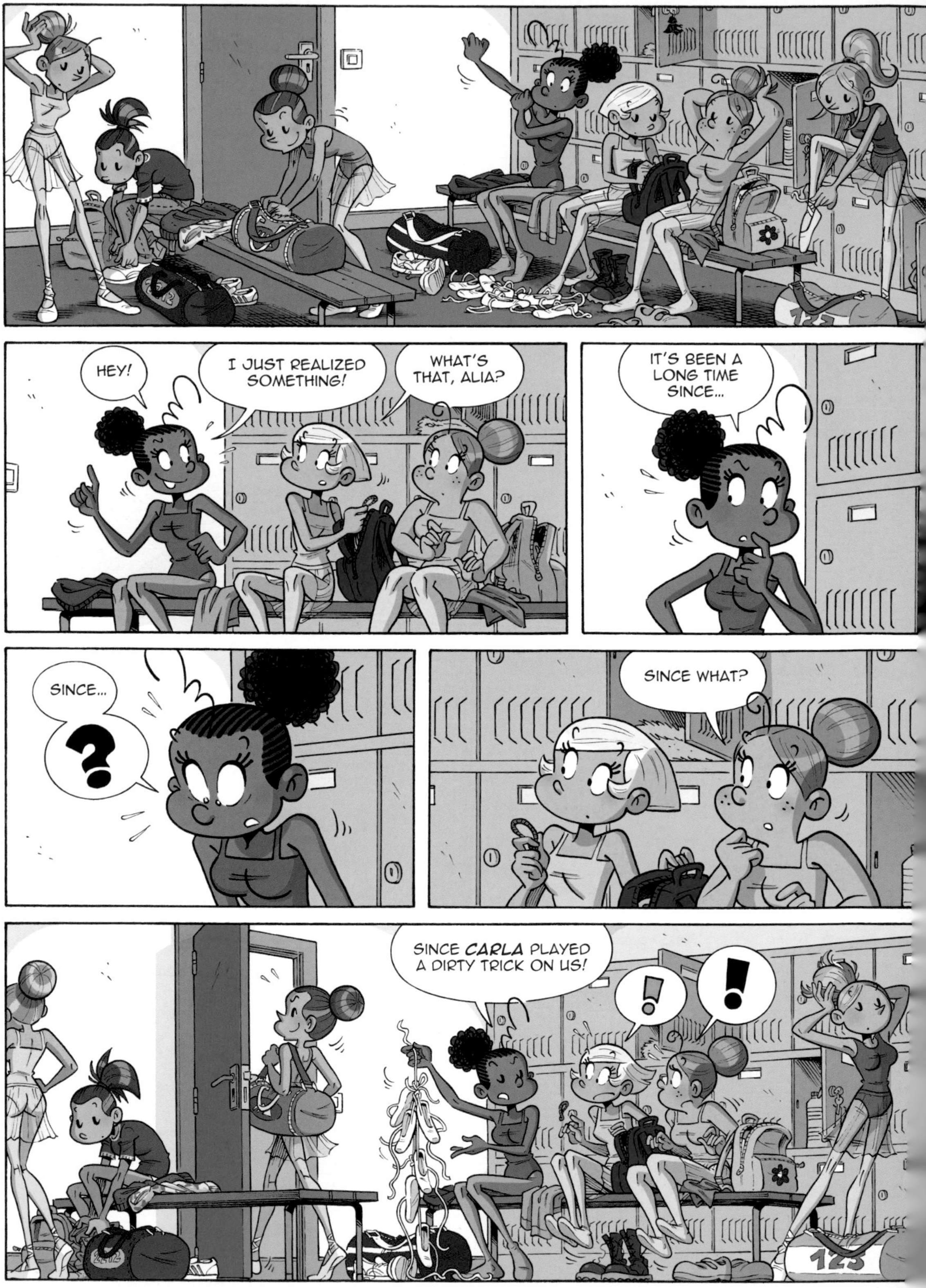
HEY!
I JUST REALIZED SOMETHING!
WHAT'S THAT, ALIA?
IT'S BEEN A LONG TIME SINCE...
SINCE...
?
SINCE WHAT?
SINCE CARLA PLAYED A DIRTY TRICK ON US!
!
!

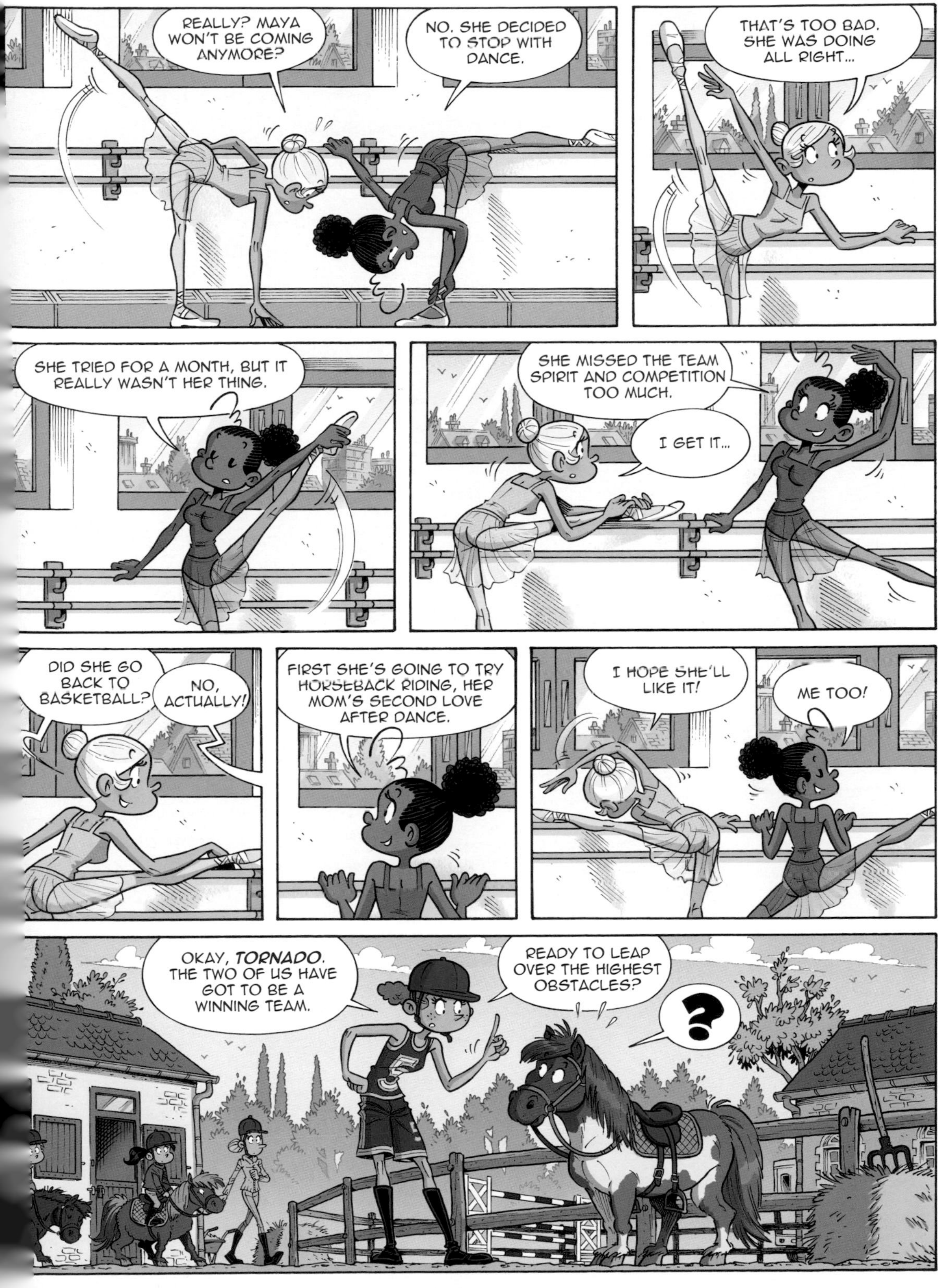
REALLY? MAYA WON'T BE COMING ANYMORE?
NO. SHE DECIDED TO STOP WITH DANCE.
THAT'S TOO BAD. SHE WAS DOING ALL RIGHT...
SHE TRIED FOR A MONTH, BUT IT REALLY WASN'T HER THING.
SHE MISSED THE TEAM SPIRIT AND COMPETITION TOO MUCH.
I GET IT...
DID SHE GO BACK TO BASKETBALL?
NO, ACTUALLY!
FIRST SHE'S GOING TO TRY HORSEBACK RIDING, HER MOM'S SECOND LOVE AFTER DANCE.
I HOPE SHE'LL LIKE IT!
ME TOO!
OKAY, **TORNADO**. THE TWO OF US HAVE GOT TO BE A WINNING TEAM.
READY TO LEAP OVER THE HIGHEST OBSTACLES?
?

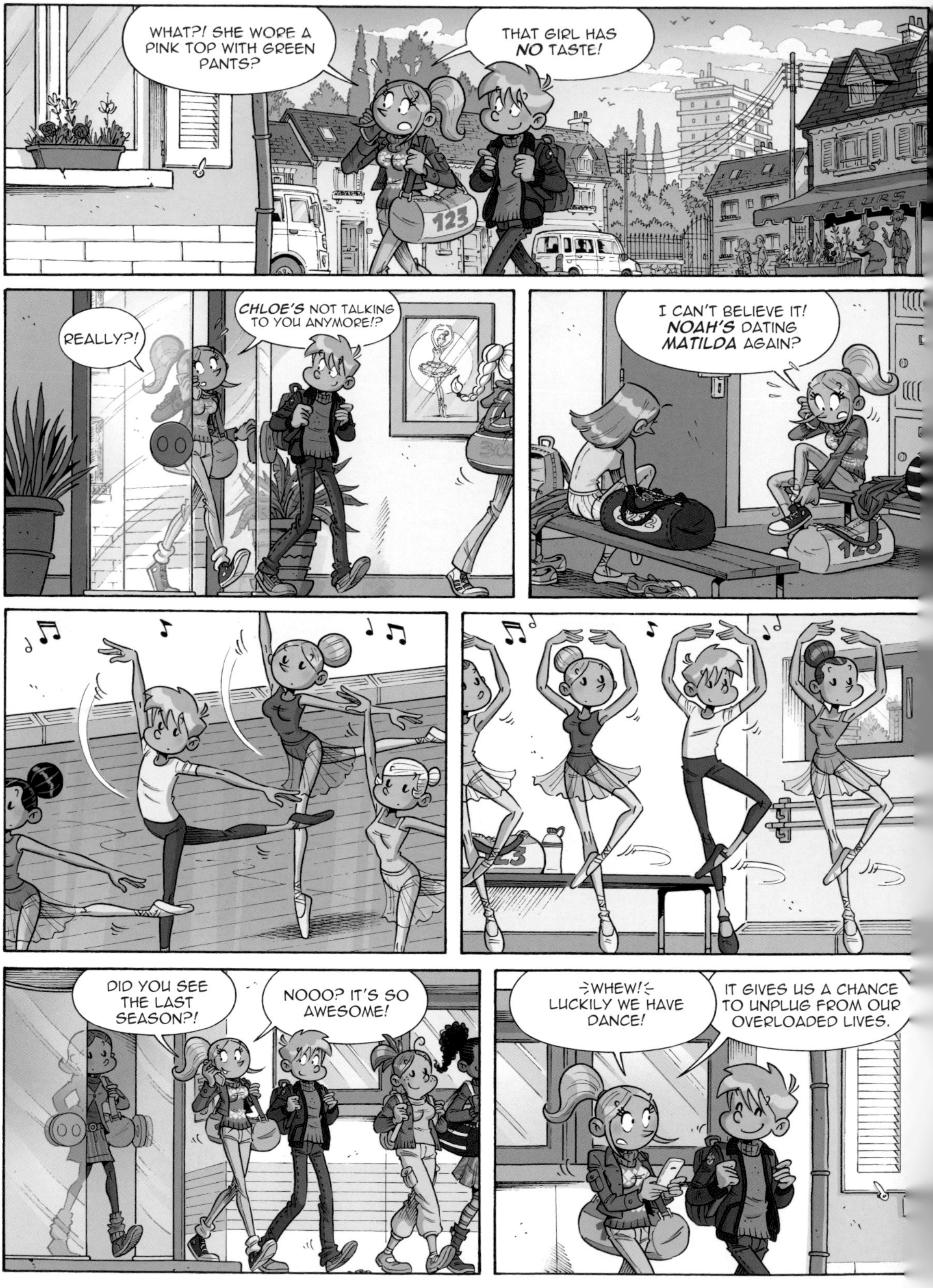
WHAT?! SHE WORE A PINK TOP WITH GREEN PANTS?
THAT GIRL HAS NO TASTE!
CHLOE'S NOT TALKING TO YOU ANYMORE!?
REALLY?!
I CAN'T BELIEVE IT! NOAH'S DATING MATILDA AGAIN?
DID YOU SEE THE LAST SEASON?!
NOOO? IT'S SO AWESOME!
WHEW! LUCKILY WE HAVE DANCE!
IT GIVES US A CHANCE TO UNPLUG FROM OUR OVERLOADED LIVES.

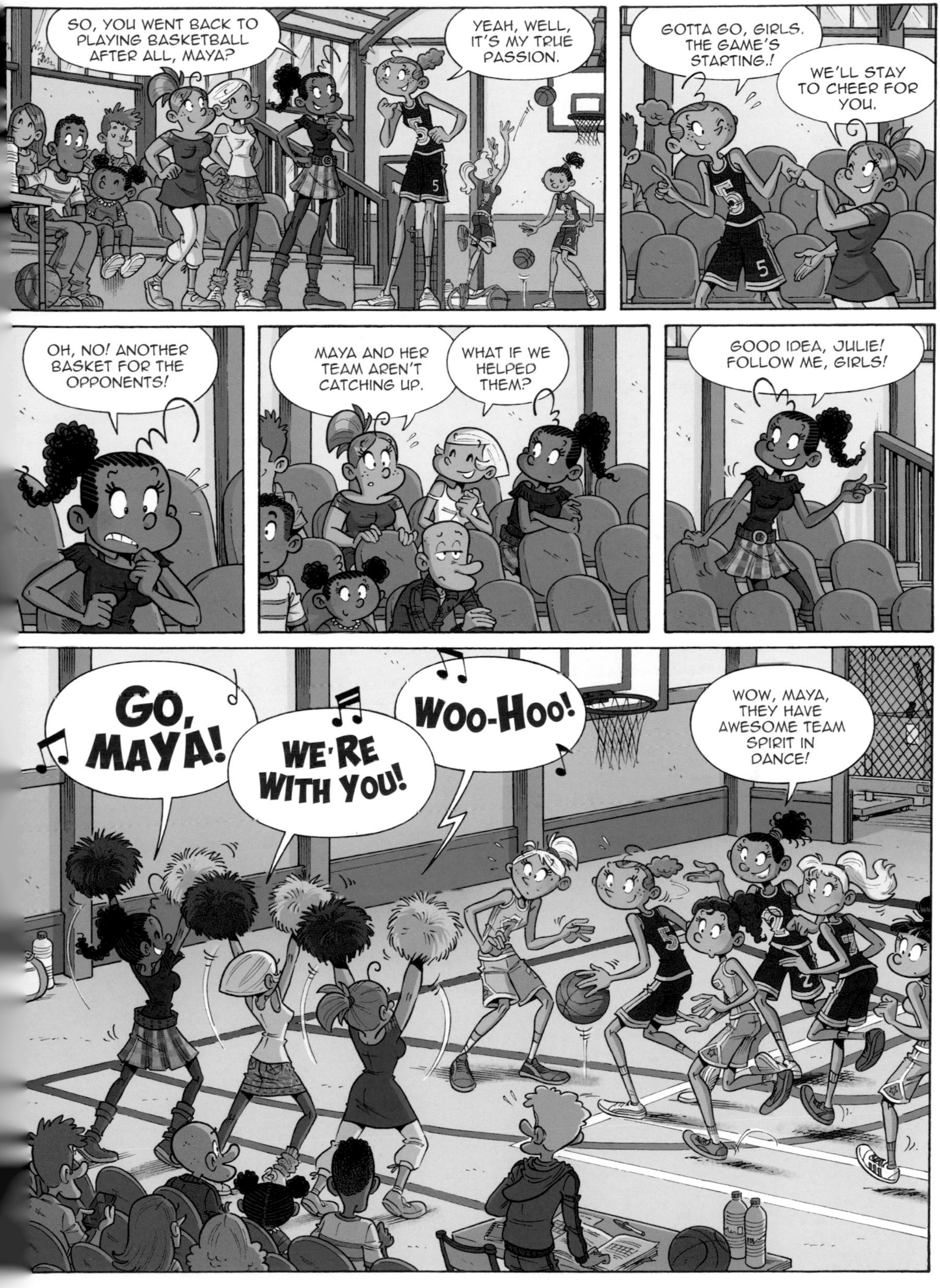
SO, YOU WENT BACK TO PLAYING BASKETBALL AFTER ALL, MAYA?
YEAH, WELL, IT'S MY TRUE PASSION.
GOTTA GO, GIRLS. THE GAME'S STARTING.!
WE'LL STAY TO CHEER FOR YOU.
OH, NO! ANOTHER BASKET FOR THE OPPONENTS!
MAYA AND HER TEAM AREN'T CATCHING UP.
WHAT IF WE HELPED THEM?
GOOD IDEA, JULIE! FOLLOW ME, GIRLS!
GO, MAYA!
WE'RE WITH YOU!
WOO-HOO!
WOW, MAYA, THEY HAVE AWESOME TEAM SPIRIT IN DANCE!

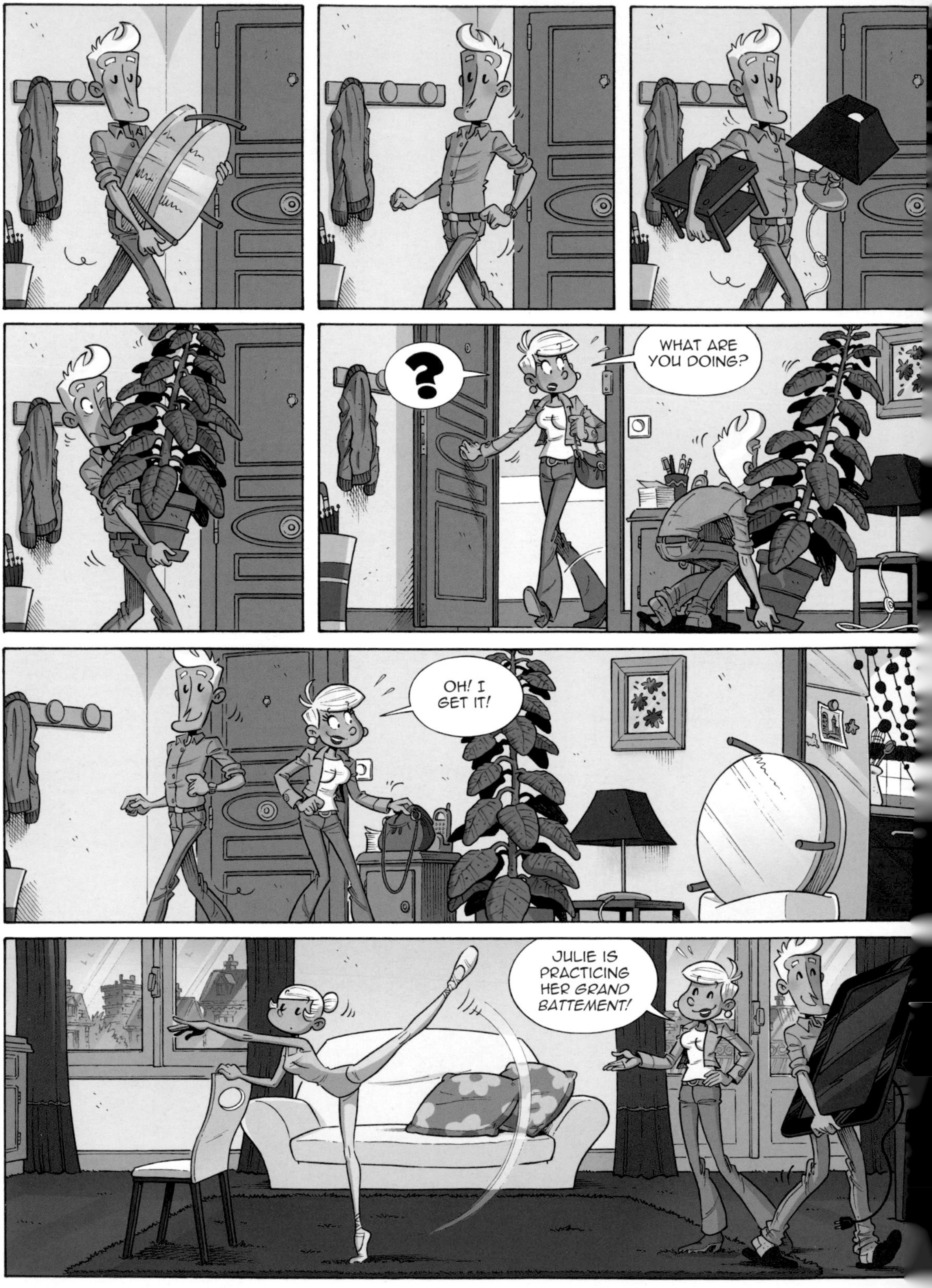
?
WHAT ARE YOU DOING?
OH! I GET IT!
JULIE IS PRACTICING HER GRAND BATTEMENT!

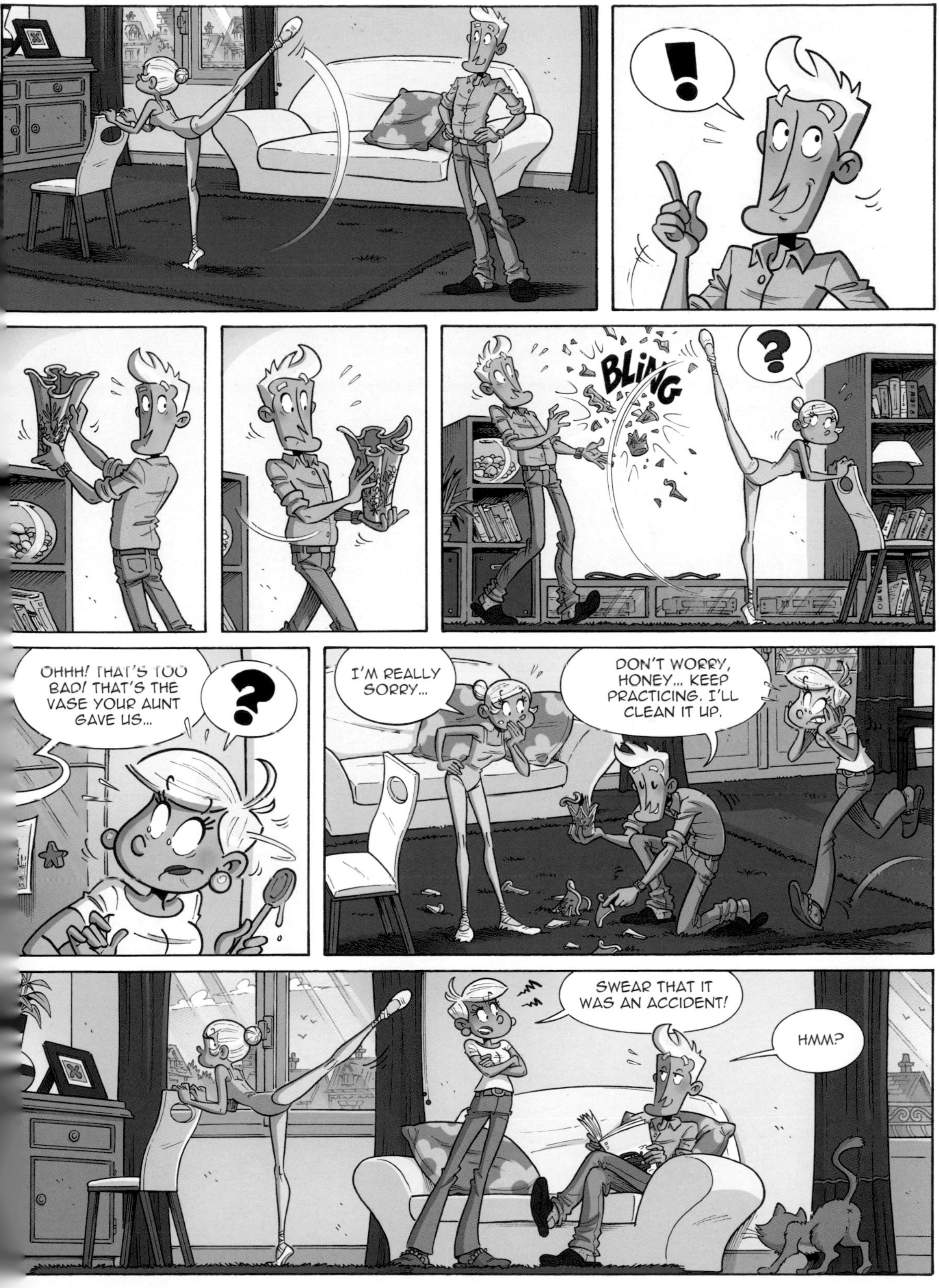
!
BLING
?
OHHH! THAT'S TOO BAD! THAT'S THE VASE YOUR AUNT GAVE US...
?
I'M REALLY SORRY...
DON'T WORRY, HONEY... KEEP PRACTICING. I'LL CLEAN IT UP.
SWEAR THAT IT WAS AN ACCIDENT!
HMM?

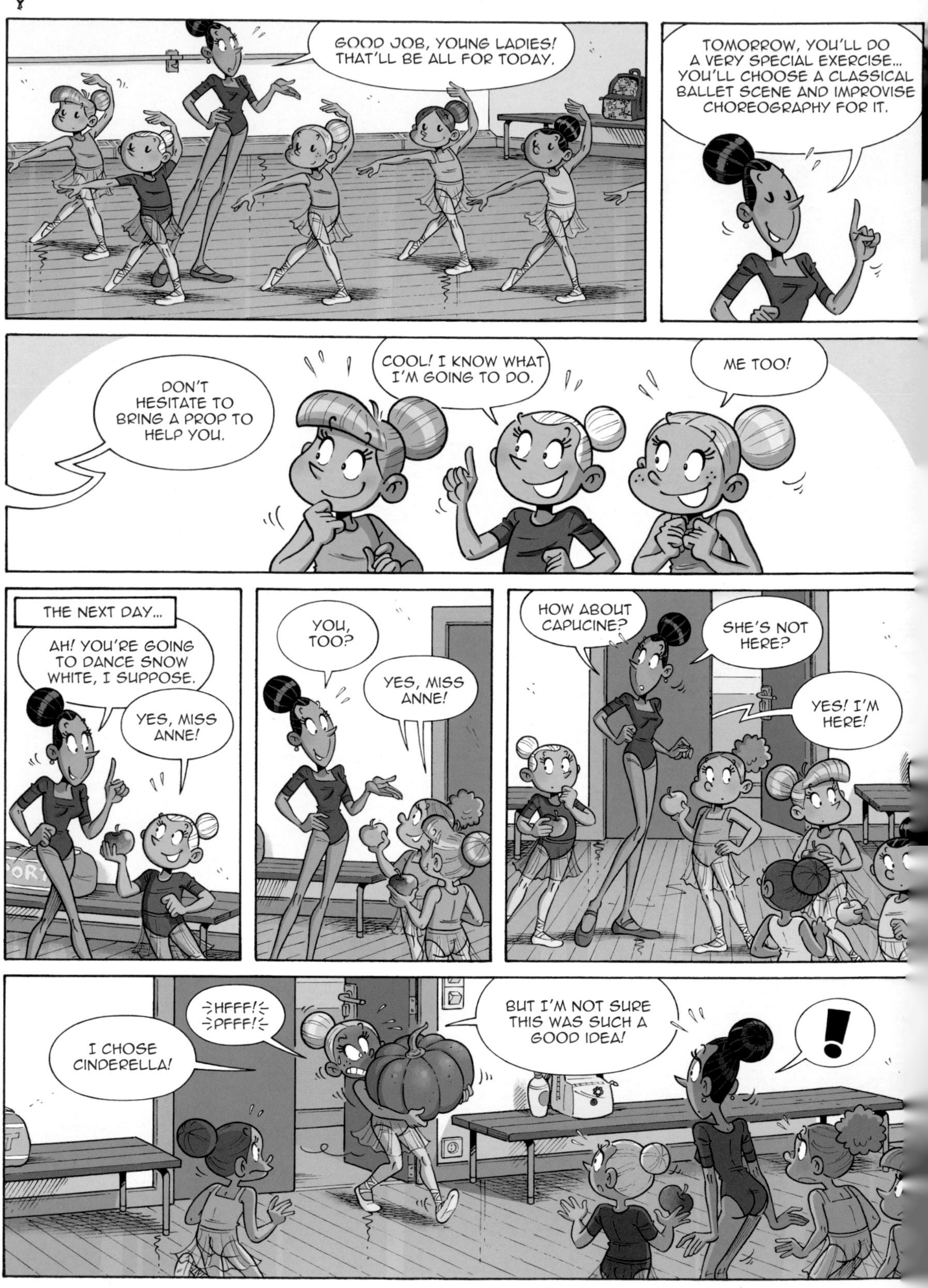
GOOD JOB, YOUNG LADIES! THAT'LL BE ALL FOR TODAY.
TOMORROW, YOU'LL DO A VERY SPECIAL EXERCISE... YOU'LL CHOOSE A CLASSICAL BALLET SCENE AND IMPROVISE CHOREOGRAPHY FOR IT.
DON'T HESITATE TO BRING A PROP TO HELP YOU.
COOL! I KNOW WHAT I'M GOING TO DO.
ME TOO!
THE NEXT DAY...
AH! YOU'RE GOING TO DANCE SNOW WHITE, I SUPPOSE.
YES, MISS ANNE!
YOU, TOO?
YES, MISS ANNE!
HOW ABOUT CAPUCINE?
SHE'S NOT HERE?
YES! I'M HERE!
I CHOSE CINDERELLA!
HFFF! PFFF!
BUT I'M NOT SURE THIS WAS SUCH A GOOD IDEA!
!

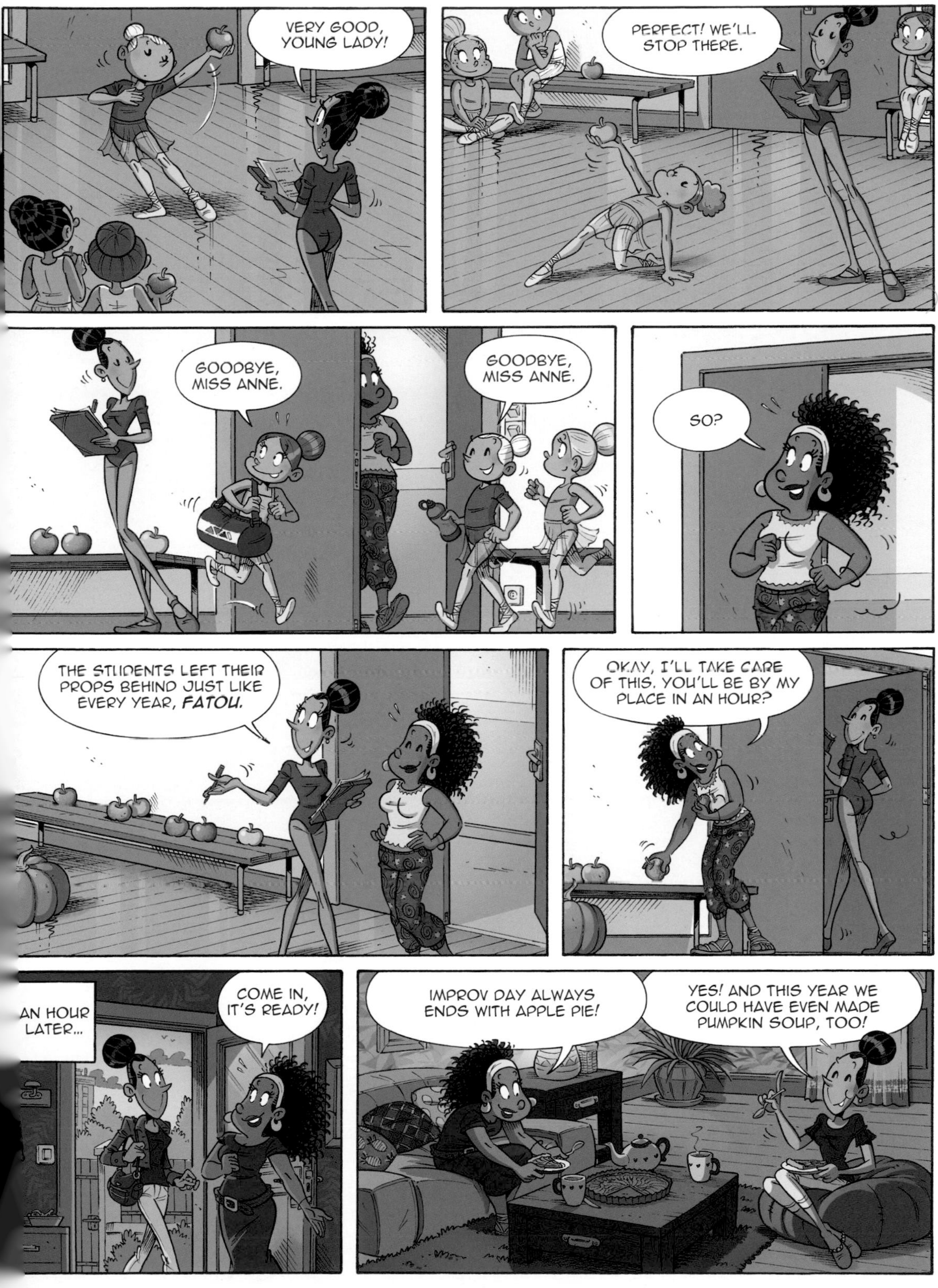
VERY GOOD, YOUNG LADY!
PERFECT! WE'LL STOP THERE.
GOODBYE, MISS ANNE.
GOODBYE, MISS ANNE.
SO?
THE STUDENTS LEFT THEIR PROPS BEHIND JUST LIKE EVERY YEAR, FATOU.
OKAY, I'LL TAKE CARE OF THIS. YOU'LL BE BY MY PLACE IN AN HOUR?
AN HOUR LATER...
COME IN, IT'S READY!
IMPROV DAY ALWAYS ENDS WITH APPLE PIE!
YES! AND THIS YEAR WE COULD HAVE EVEN MADE PUMPKIN SOUP, TOO!

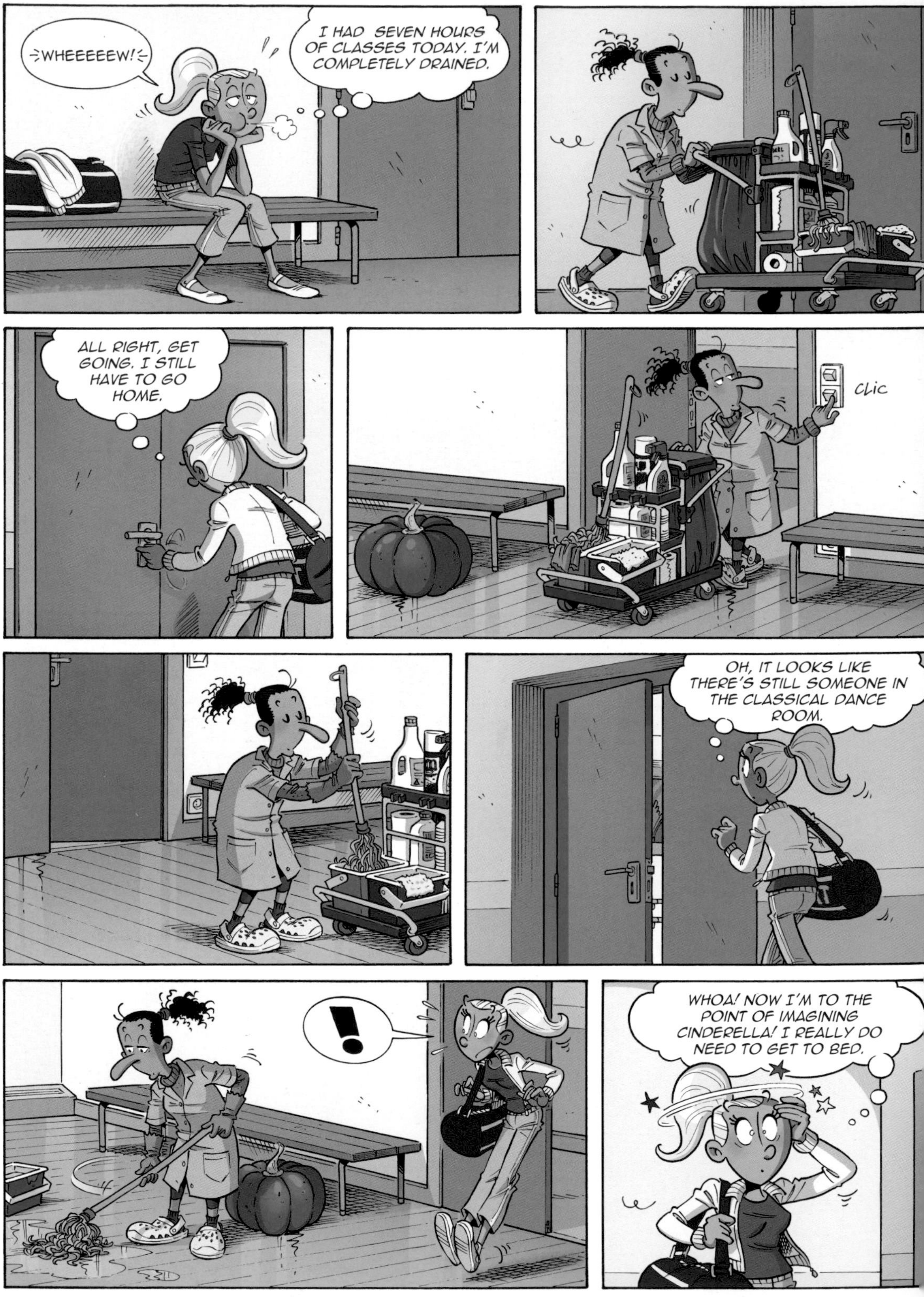
WHEEEEEW!
I HAD SEVEN HOURS OF CLASSES TODAY. I'M COMPLETELY DRAINED.
ALL RIGHT, GET GOING. I STILL HAVE TO GO HOME.
CLIC
OH, IT LOOKS LIKE THERE'S STILL SOMEONE IN THE CLASSICAL DANCE ROOM.
!
WHOA! NOW I'M TO THE POINT OF IMAGINING CINDERELLA! I REALLY DO NEED TO GET TO BED.

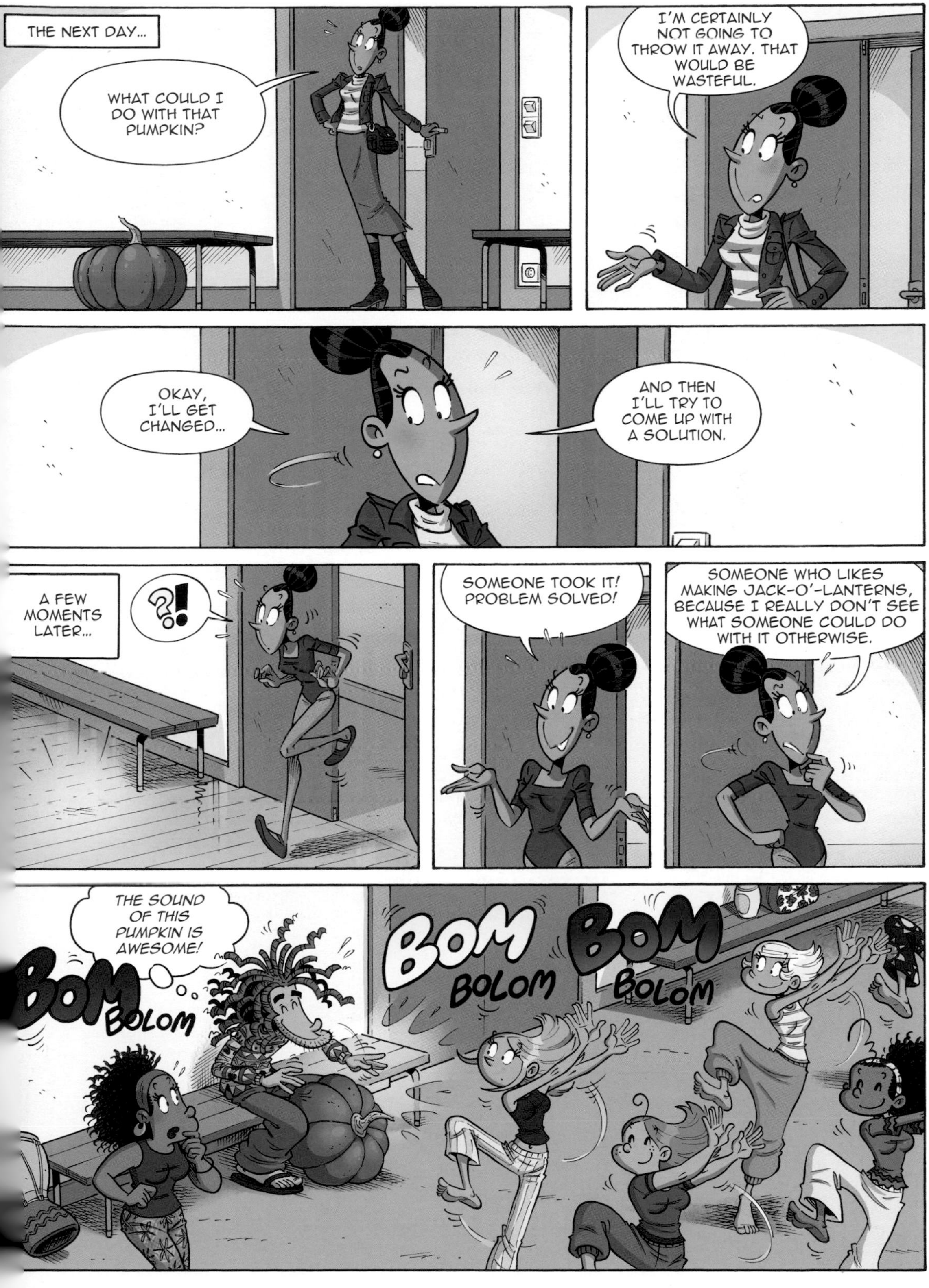
THE NEXT DAY...
WHAT COULD I DO WITH THAT PUMPKIN?
I'M CERTAINLY NOT GOING TO THROW IT AWAY. THAT WOULD BE WASTEFUL.
OKAY, I'LL GET CHANGED...
AND THEN I'LL TRY TO COME UP WITH A SOLUTION.
A FEW MOMENTS LATER...
?!
SOMEONE TOOK IT! PROBLEM SOLVED!
SOMEONE WHO LIKES MAKING JACK-O'-LANTERNS, BECAUSE I REALLY DON'T SEE WHAT SOMEONE COULD DO WITH IT OTHERWISE.
THE SOUND OF THIS PUMPKIN IS AWESOME!
BOM BOLOM
BOM BOLOM
BOM BOLOM

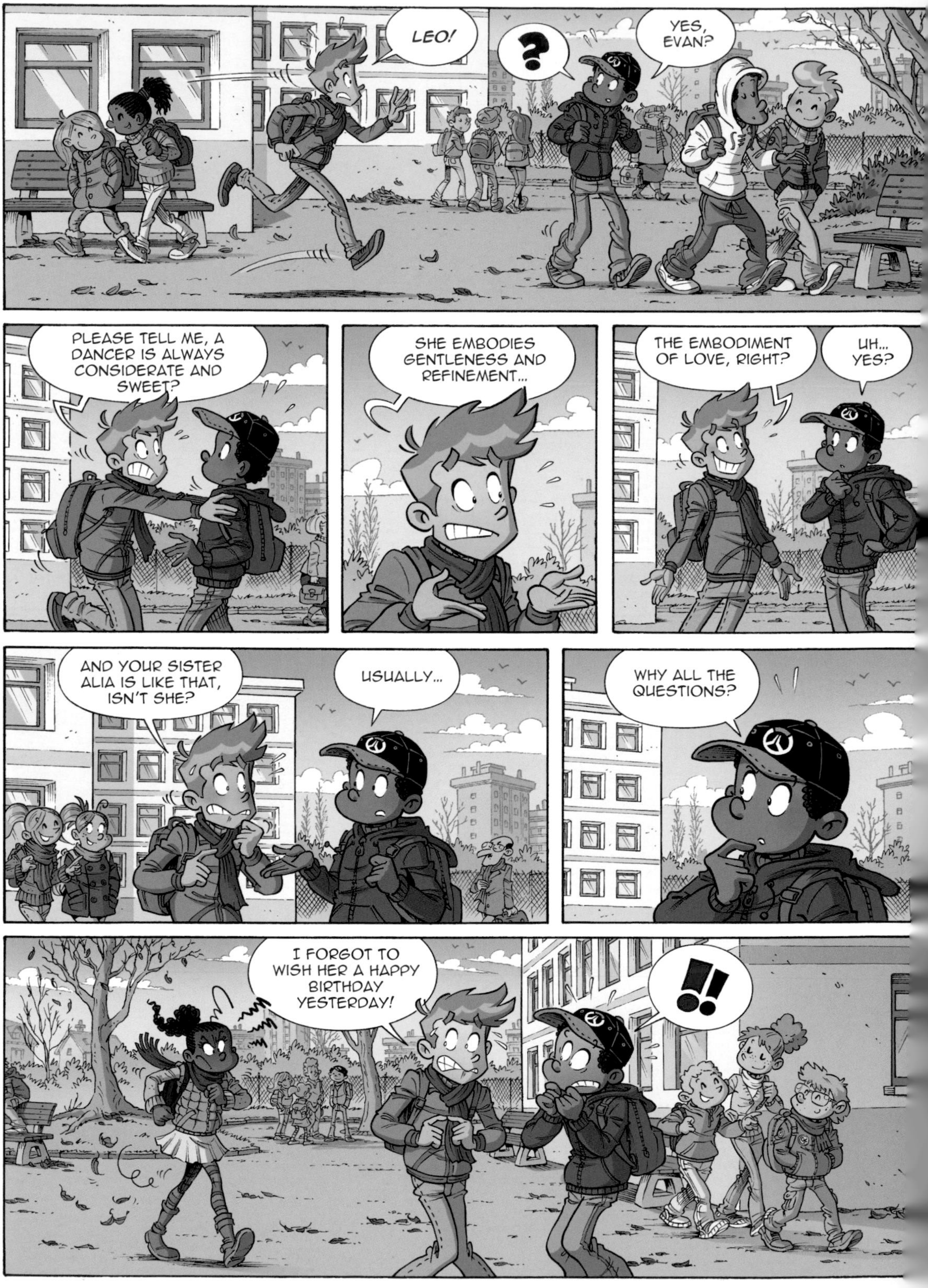
LEO!
?
YES, EVAN?
PLEASE TELL ME, A DANCER IS ALWAYS CONSIDERATE AND SWEET?
SHE EMBODIES GENTLENESS AND REFINEMENT...
THE EMBODIMENT OF LOVE, RIGHT?
UH... YES?
AND YOUR SISTER ALIA IS LIKE THAT, ISN'T SHE?
USUALLY...
WHY ALL THE QUESTIONS?
I FORGOT TO WISH HER A HAPPY BIRTHDAY YESTERDAY!
!!

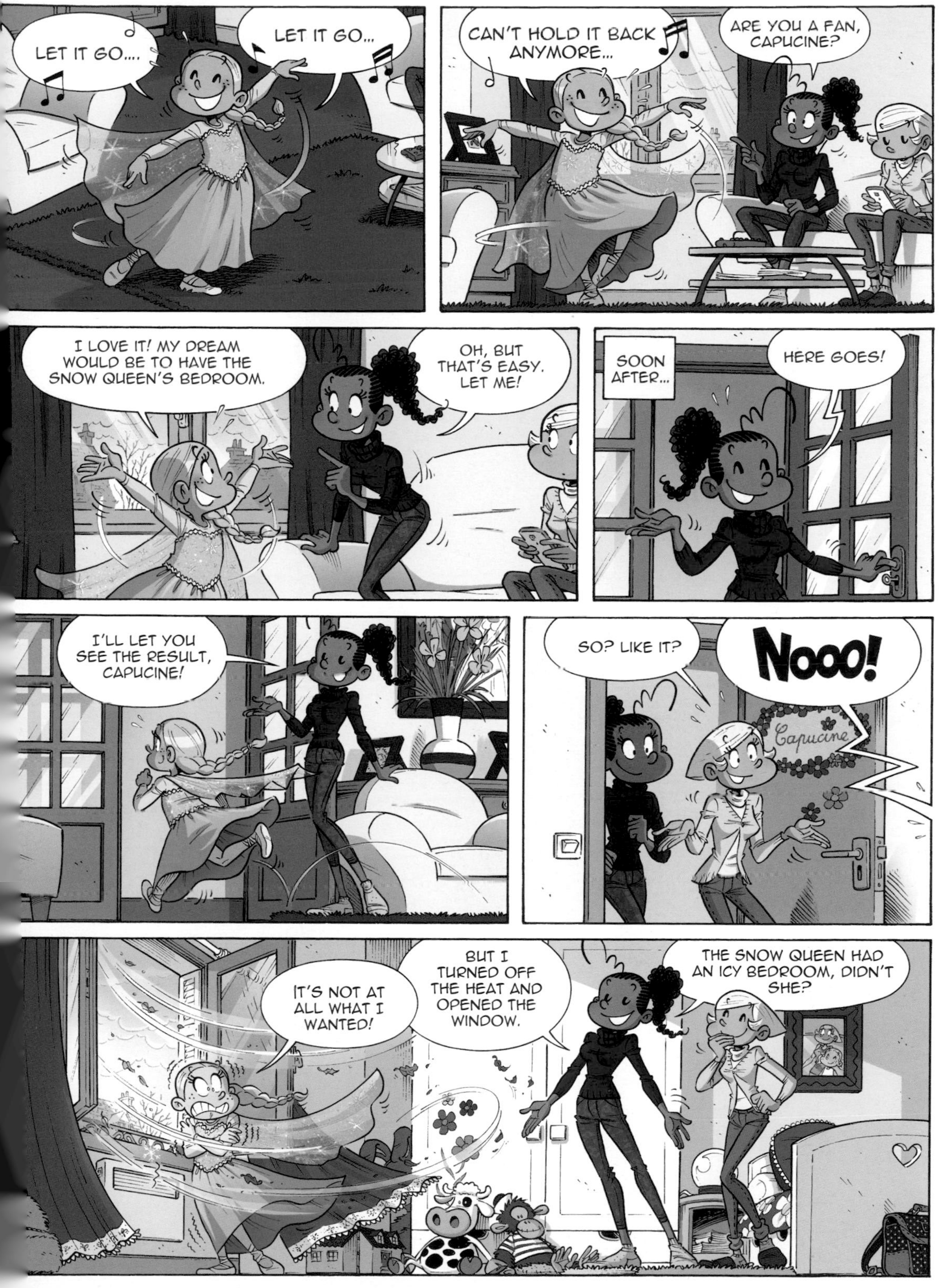
LET IT GO....
LET IT GO...
CAN'T HOLD IT BACK ANYMORE...
ARE YOU A FAN, CAPUCINE?
I LOVE IT! MY DREAM WOULD BE TO HAVE THE SNOW QUEEN'S BEDROOM.
OH, BUT THAT'S EASY. LET ME!
SOON AFTER...
HERE GOES!
I'LL LET YOU SEE THE RESULT, CAPUCINE!
SO? LIKE IT?
NOOO!
Capucine
IT'S NOT AT ALL WHAT I WANTED!
BUT I TURNED OFF THE HEAT AND OPENED THE WINDOW.
THE SNOW QUEEN HAD AN ICY BEDROOM, DIDN'T SHE?

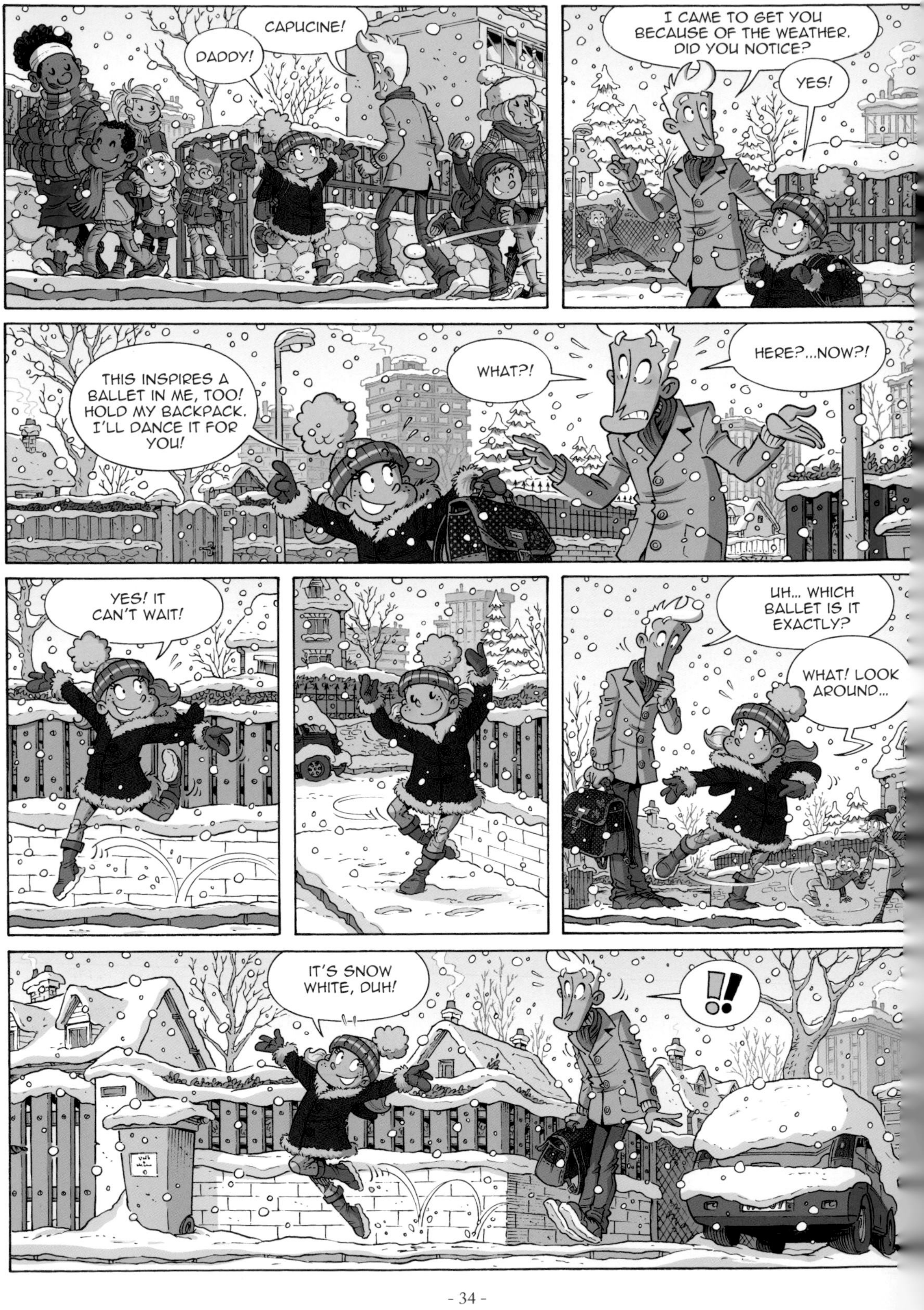
CAPUCINE!
DADDY!
I CAME TO GET YOU BECAUSE OF THE WEATHER. DID YOU NOTICE?
YES!
THIS INSPIRES A BALLET IN ME, TOO! HOLD MY BACKPACK. I'LL DANCE IT FOR YOU!
WHAT?!
HERE?...NOW?!
YES! IT CAN'T WAIT!
UH... WHICH BALLET IS IT EXACTLY?
WHAT! LOOK AROUND...
IT'S SNOW WHITE, DUH!
!!

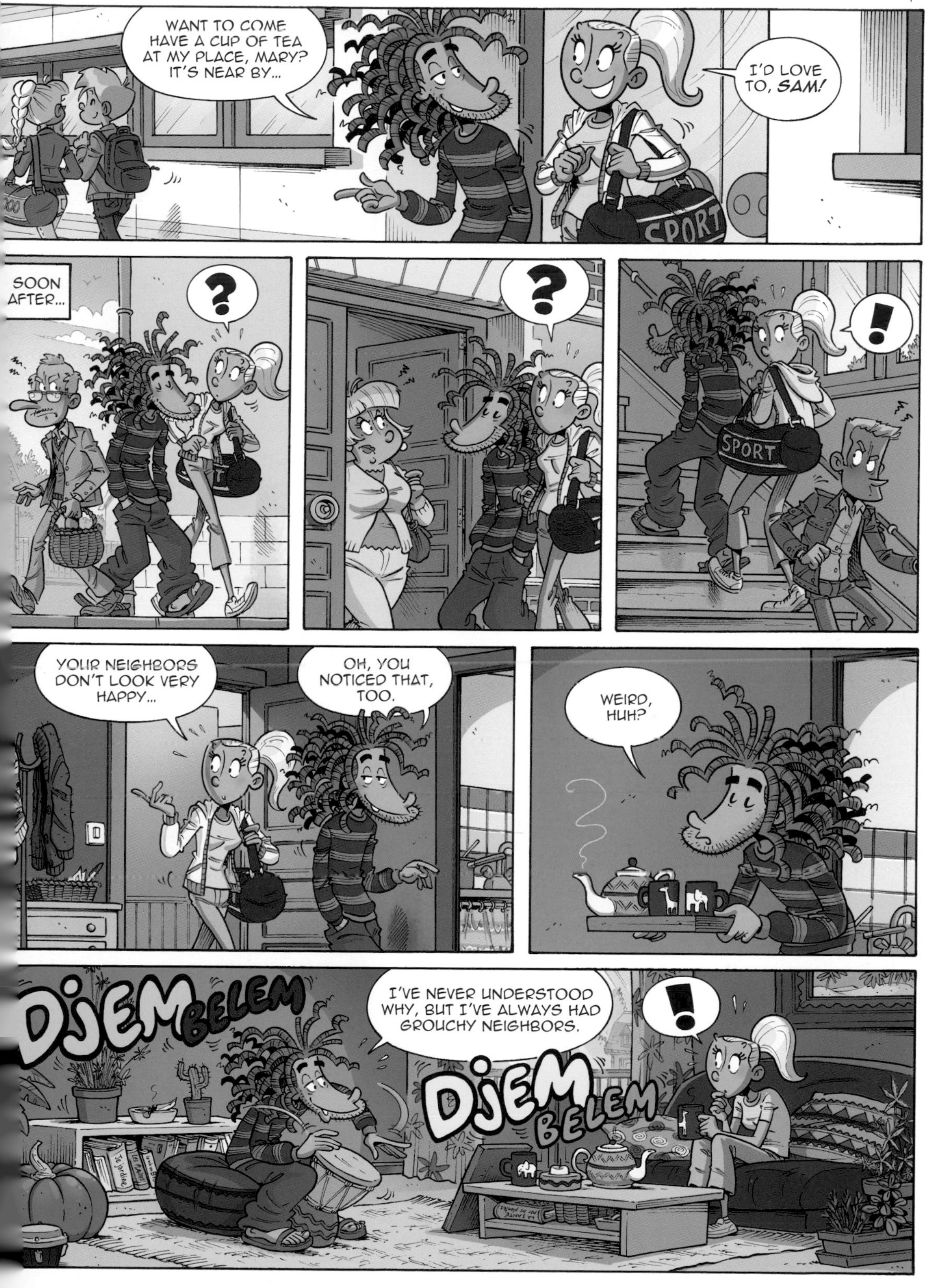
WANT TO COME HAVE A CUP OF TEA AT MY PLACE, MARY? IT'S NEAR BY...
I'D LOVE TO, SAM!
SPORT
SOON AFTER...
?
?
!
SPORT
YOUR NEIGHBORS DON'T LOOK VERY HAPPY...
OH, YOU NOTICED THAT, TOO.
WEIRD, HUH?
DJEM BELEM
I'VE NEVER UNDERSTOOD WHY, BUT I'VE ALWAYS HAD GROUCHY NEIGHBORS.
!
DJEM BELEM

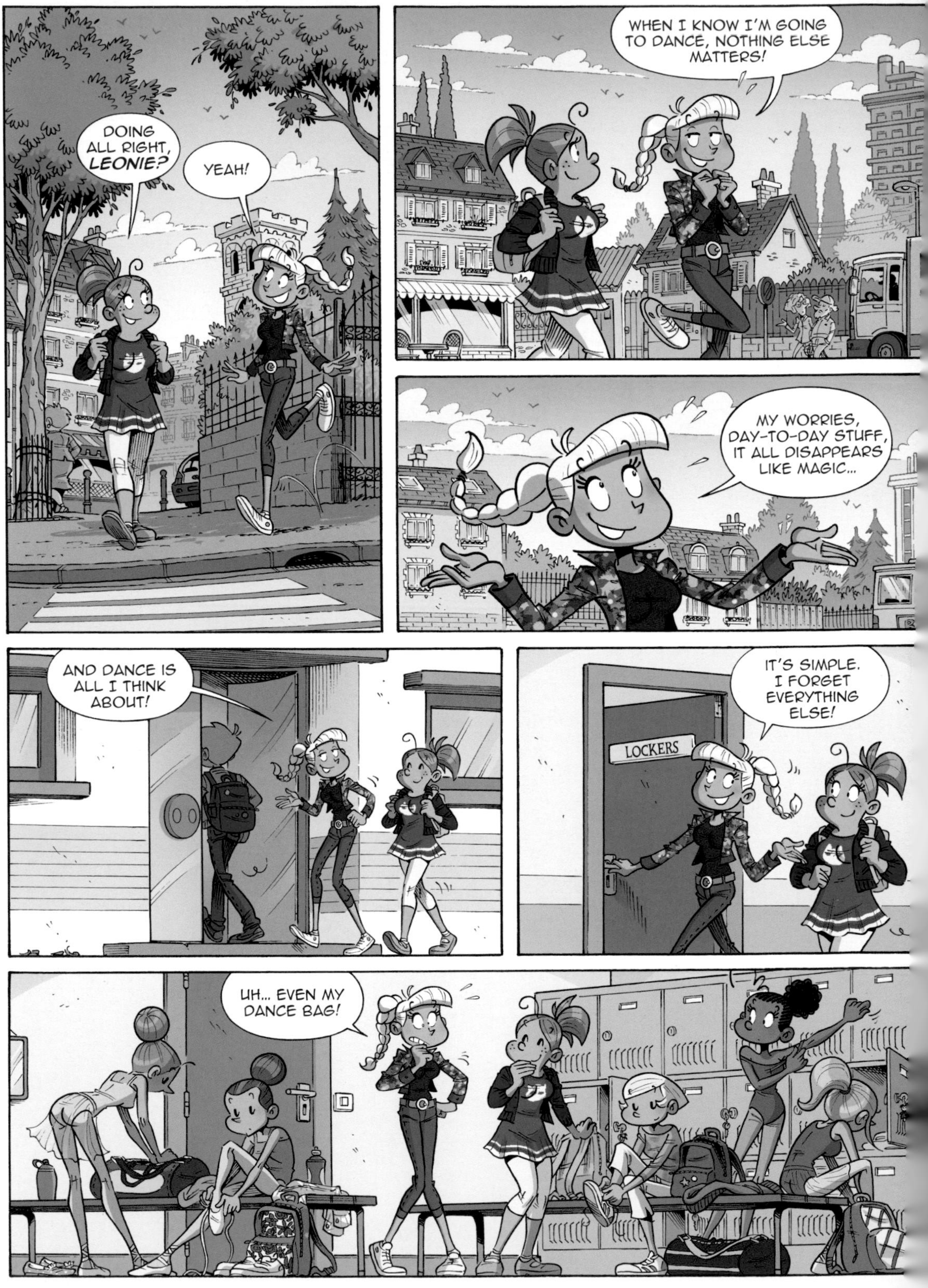
DOING ALL RIGHT, LEONIE?
YEAH!
WHEN I KNOW I'M GOING TO DANCE, NOTHING ELSE MATTERS!
MY WORRIES, DAY-TO-DAY STUFF, IT ALL DISAPPEARS LIKE MAGIC...
AND DANCE IS ALL I THINK ABOUT!
LOCKERS
IT'S SIMPLE. I FORGET EVERYTHING ELSE!
UH... EVEN MY DANCE BAG!

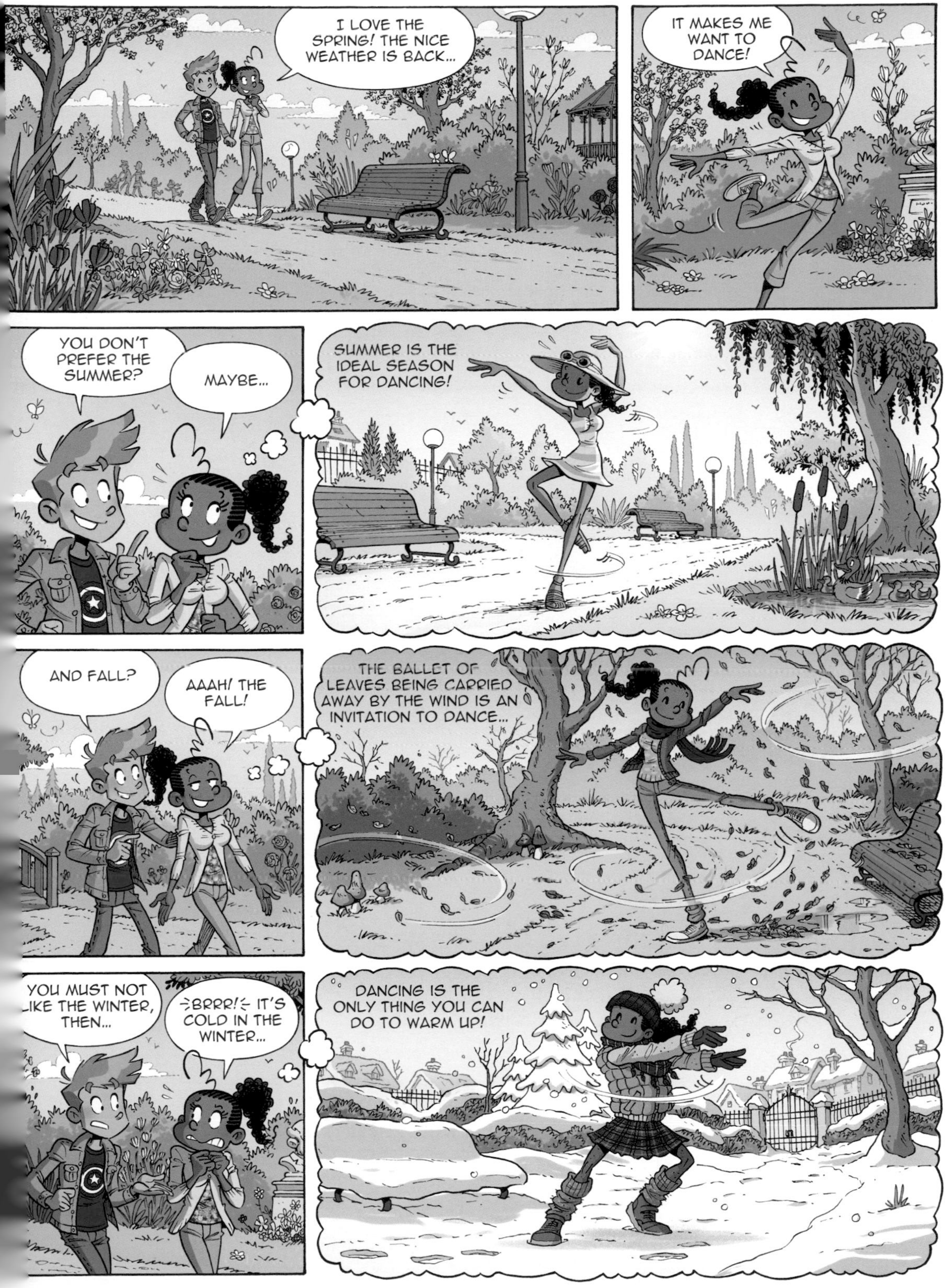
I LOVE THE SPRING! THE NICE WEATHER IS BACK...
IT MAKES ME WANT TO DANCE!
YOU DON'T PREFER THE SUMMER?
MAYBE...
SUMMER IS THE IDEAL SEASON FOR DANCING!
AND FALL?
AAAH! THE FALL!
THE BALLET OF LEAVES BEING CARRIED AWAY BY THE WIND IS AN INVITATION TO DANCE...
YOU MUST NOT LIKE THE WINTER, THEN...
BRRR! IT'S COLD IN THE WINTER...
DANCING IS THE ONLY THING YOU CAN DO TO WARM UP!

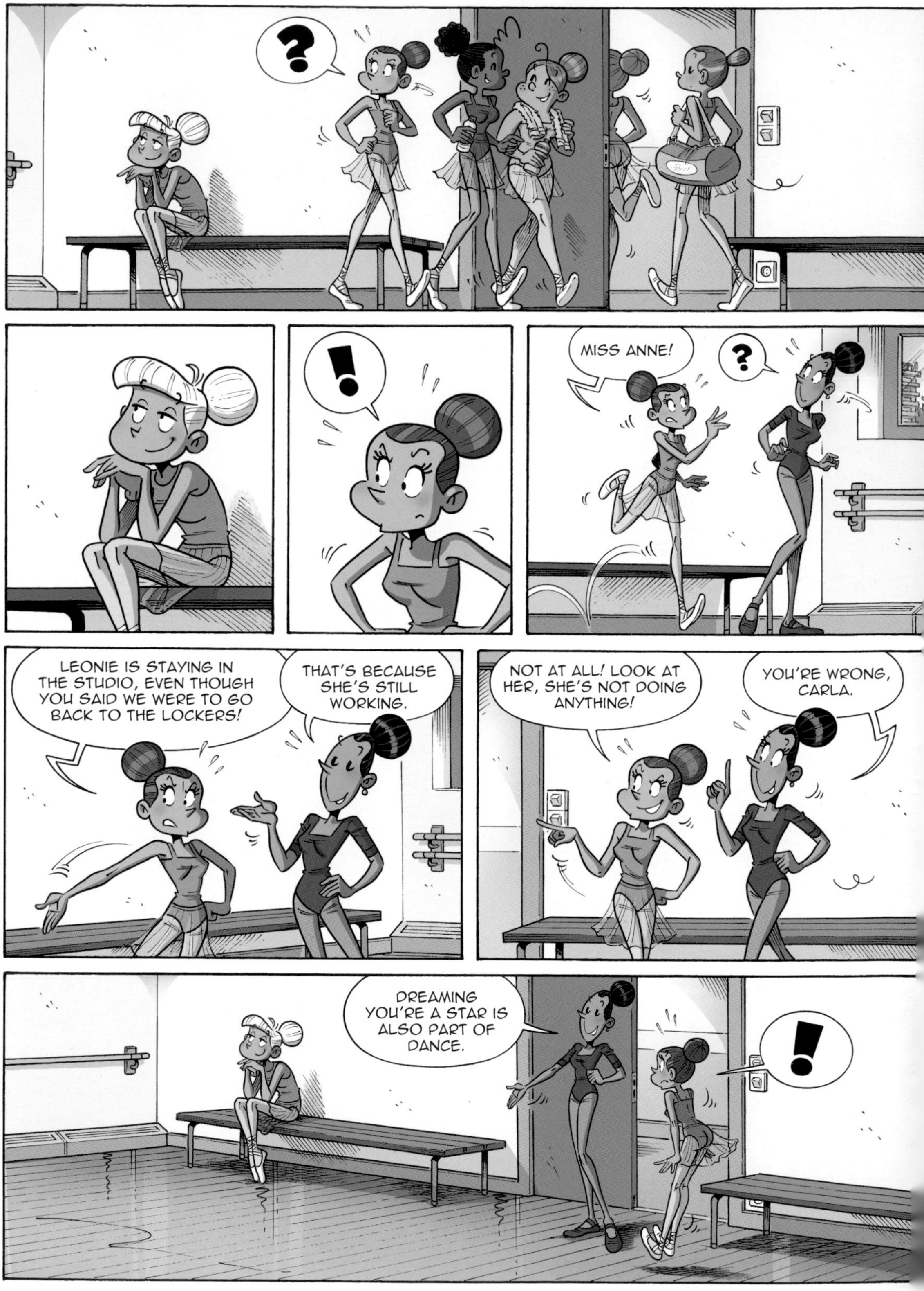
?
!
MISS ANNE!
?
LEONIE IS STAYING IN THE STUDIO, EVEN THOUGH YOU SAID WE WERE TO GO BACK TO THE LOCKERS!
THAT'S BECAUSE SHE'S STILL WORKING.
NOT AT ALL! LOOK AT HER, SHE'S NOT DOING ANYTHING!
YOU'RE WRONG, CARLA.
DREAMING YOU'RE A STAR IS ALSO PART OF DANCE.
!

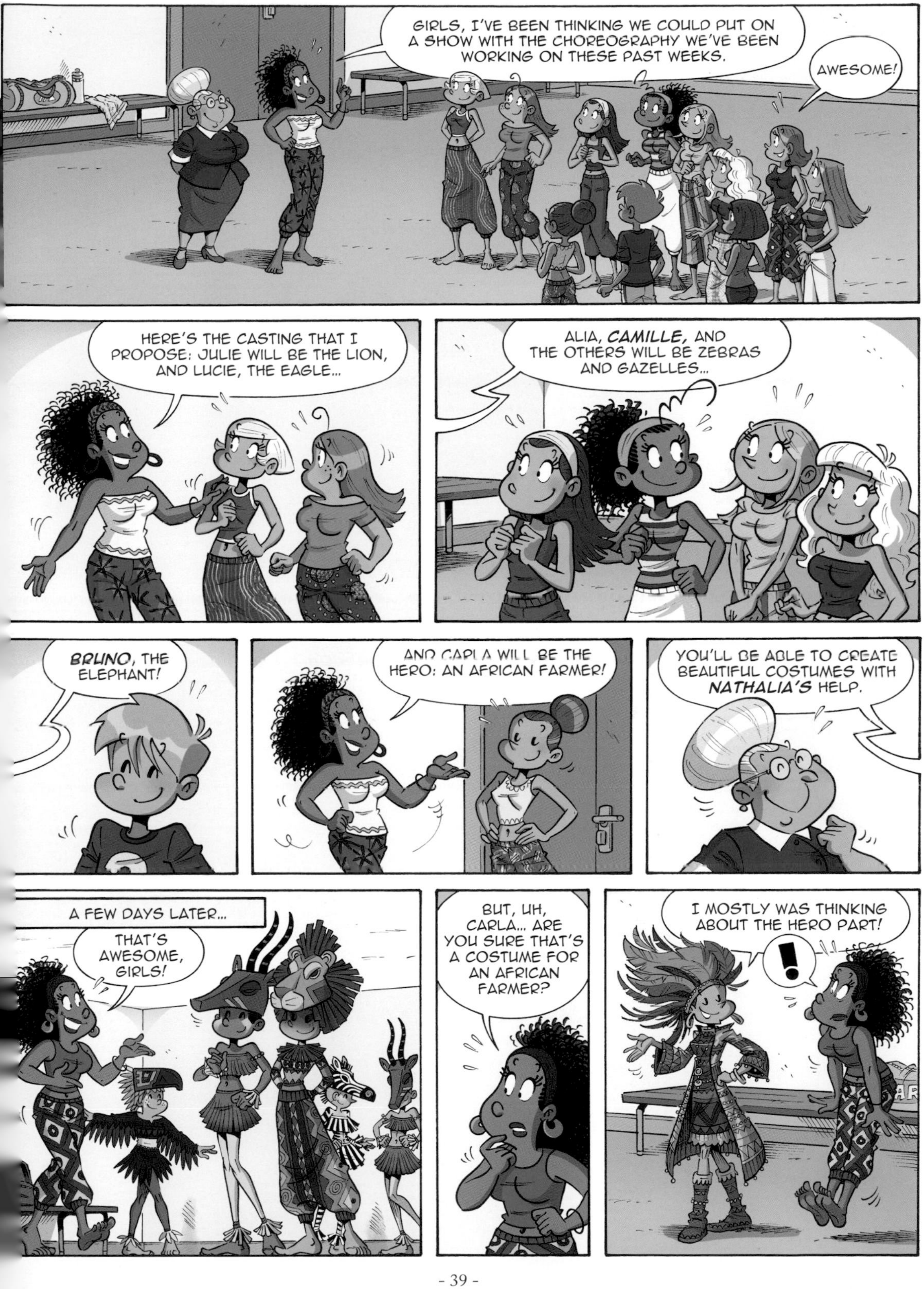
GIRLS, I'VE BEEN THINKING WE COULD PUT ON A SHOW WITH THE CHOREOGRAPHY WE'VE BEEN WORKING ON THESE PAST WEEKS.
AWESOME!
HERE'S THE CASTING THAT I PROPOSE: JULIE WILL BE THE LION, AND LUCIE, THE EAGLE...
ALIA, CAMILLE, AND THE OTHERS WILL BE ZEBRAS AND GAZELLES...
BRUNO, THE ELEPHANT!
AND CARLA WILL BE THE HERO: AN AFRICAN FARMER!
YOU'LL BE ABLE TO CREATE BEAUTIFUL COSTUMES WITH NATHALIA'S HELP.
A FEW DAYS LATER...
THAT'S AWESOME, GIRLS!
BUT, UH, CARLA... ARE YOU SURE THAT'S A COSTUME FOR AN AFRICAN FARMER?
I MOSTLY WAS THINKING ABOUT THE HERO PART!
!

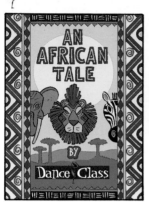

AN AFRICAN TALE
BY
Dance Class

AN AFRICAN FARMER WANTS TO FARM A NEW FIELD. SO HE GOES TO THE KINGDOM OF THE ANIMALS...

WITH THE SECRET PLAN OF MAKING THEM WORK FOR HIM...

BEM BELEM

BEM BELEM

BEM BELEM

BEM BELEM

BEM

CLAP CLAP CLAP

OHHH! I LOVE THAT SCENE WHERE CARLA BOWS TO US!

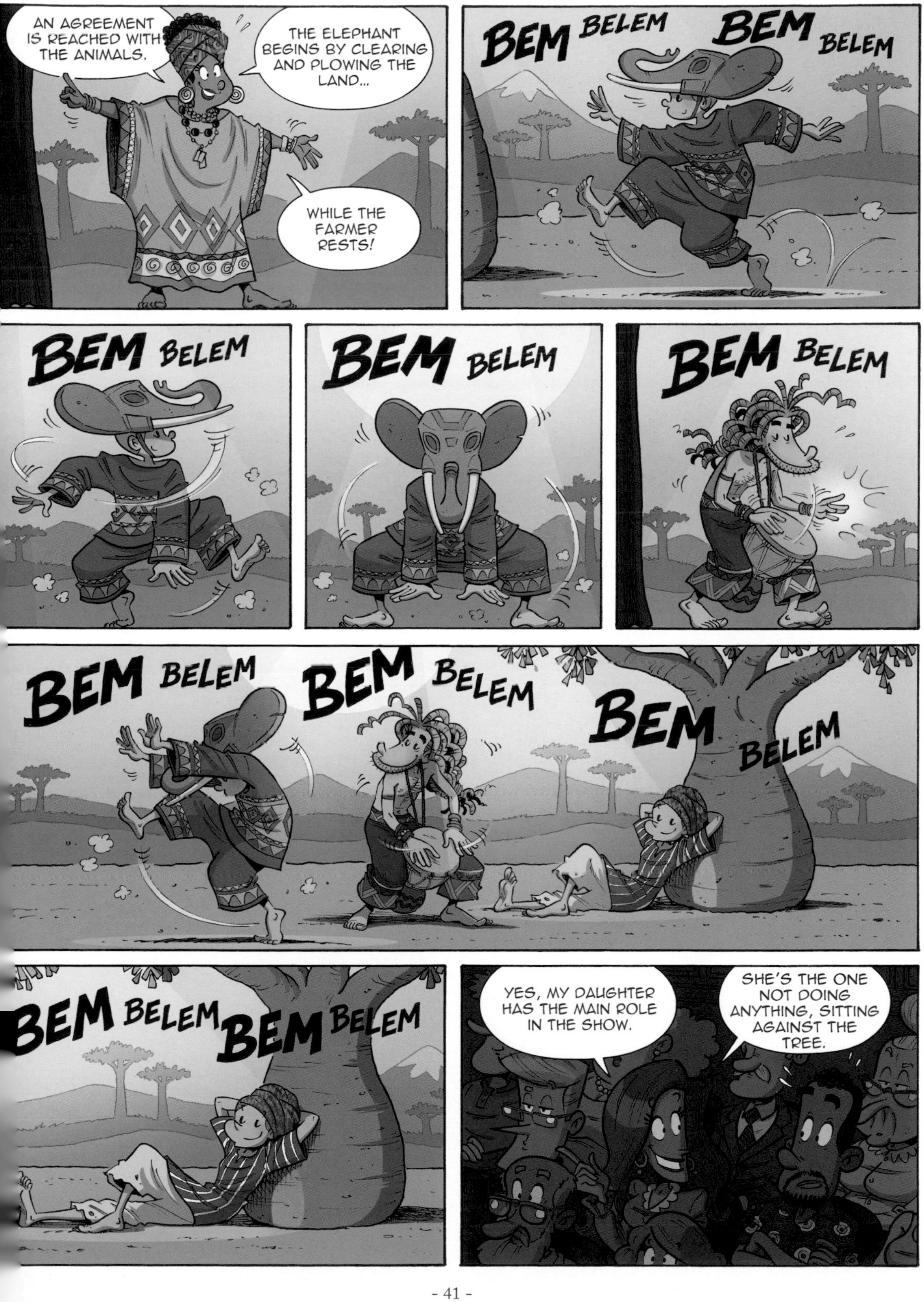
AN AGREEMENT IS REACHED WITH THE ANIMALS.
THE ELEPHANT BEGINS BY CLEARING AND PLOWING THE LAND...
WHILE THE FARMER RESTS!
BEM BELEM BEM BELEM
BEM BELEM
BEM BELEM
BEM BELEM
BEM BELEM BEM BELEM BEM BELEM
BEM BELEM BEM BELEM
YES, MY DAUGHTER HAS THE MAIN ROLE IN THE SHOW.
SHE'S THE ONE NOT DOING ANYTHING, SITTING AGAINST THE TREE.

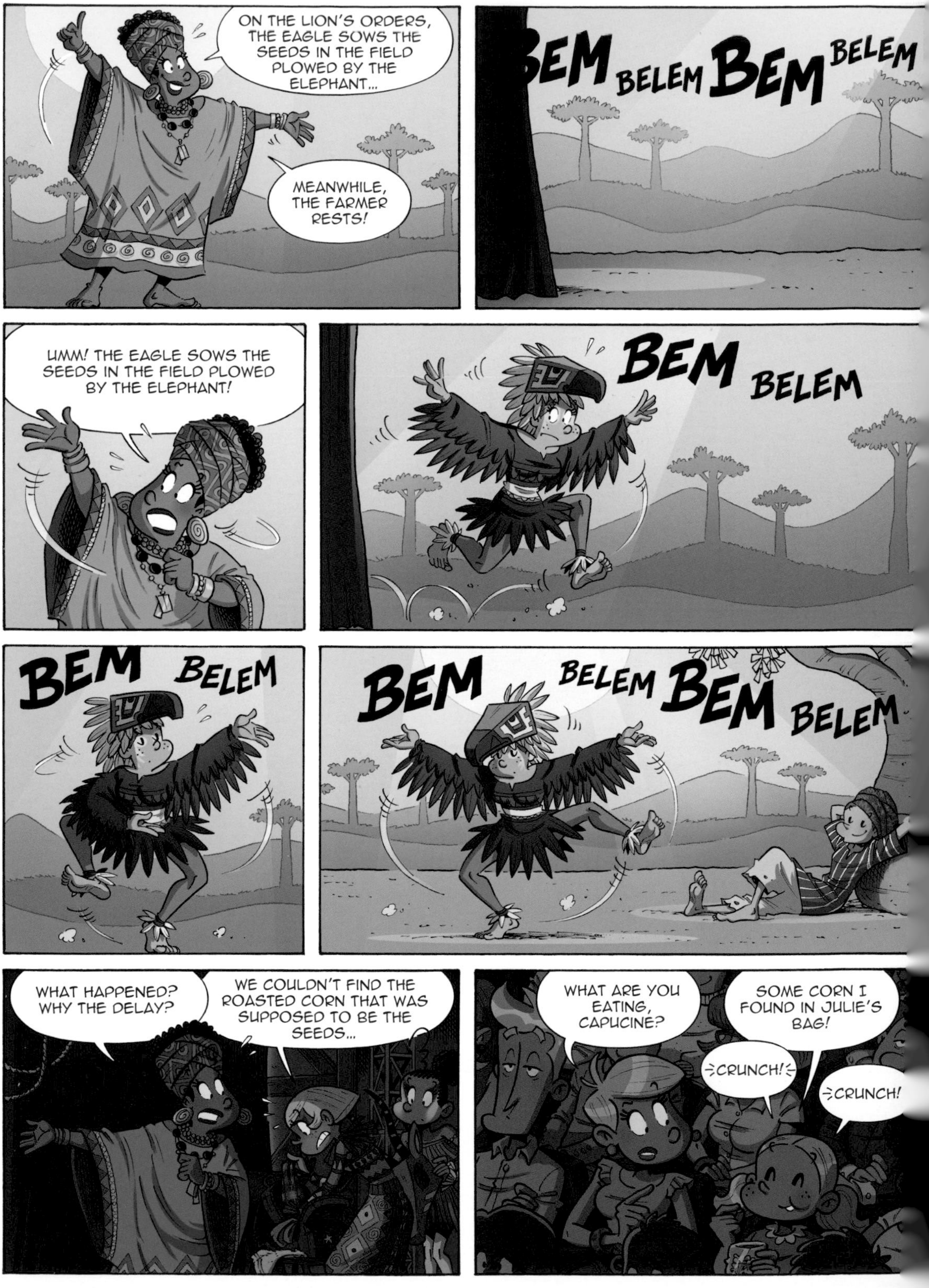

ON THE LION'S ORDERS, THE EAGLE SOWS THE SEEDS IN THE FIELD PLOWED BY THE ELEPHANT...
MEANWHILE, THE FARMER RESTS!
BEM BELEM BEM BELEM
UMM! THE EAGLE SOWS THE SEEDS IN THE FIELD PLOWED BY THE ELEPHANT!
BEM BELEM
BEM BELEM
BEM BELEM BEM BELEM
WHAT HAPPENED? WHY THE DELAY?
WE COULDN'T FIND THE ROASTED CORN THAT WAS SUPPOSED TO BE THE SEEDS...
WHAT ARE YOU EATING, CAPUCINE?
SOME CORN I FOUND IN JULIE'S BAG!
CRUNCH!
CRUNCH!

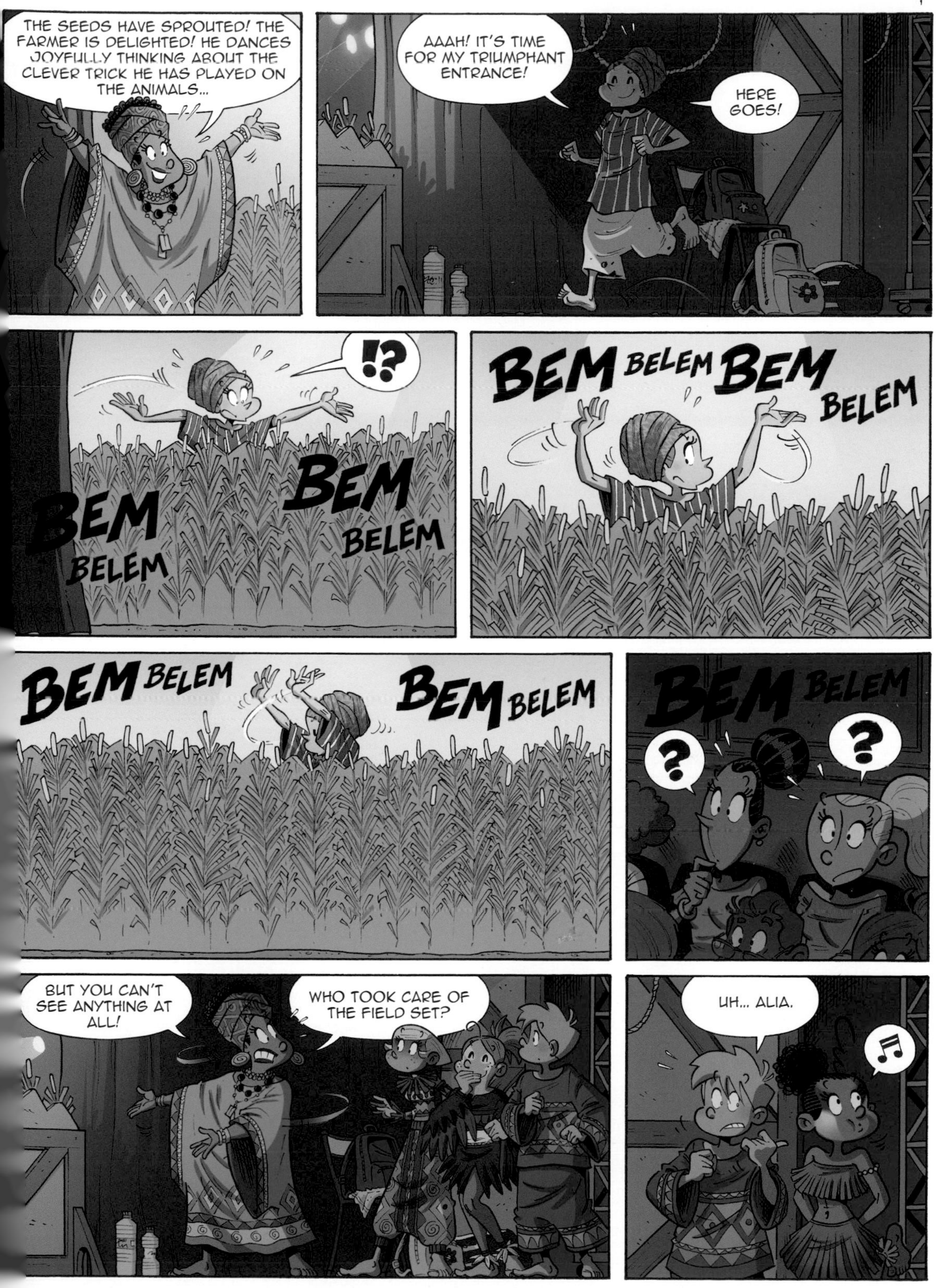
THE SEEDS HAVE SPROUTED! THE FARMER IS DELIGHTED! HE DANCES JOYFULLY THINKING ABOUT THE CLEVER TRICK HE HAS PLAYED ON THE ANIMALS...
AAAH! IT'S TIME FOR MY TRIUMPHANT ENTRANCE!
HERE GOES!
!?
BEM BELEM BEM BELEM
BEM BELEM BEM BELEM
BEM BELEM BEM BELEM
BEM BELEM
?
?
BUT YOU CAN'T SEE ANYTHING AT ALL!
WHO TOOK CARE OF THE FIELD SET?
UH... ALIA.

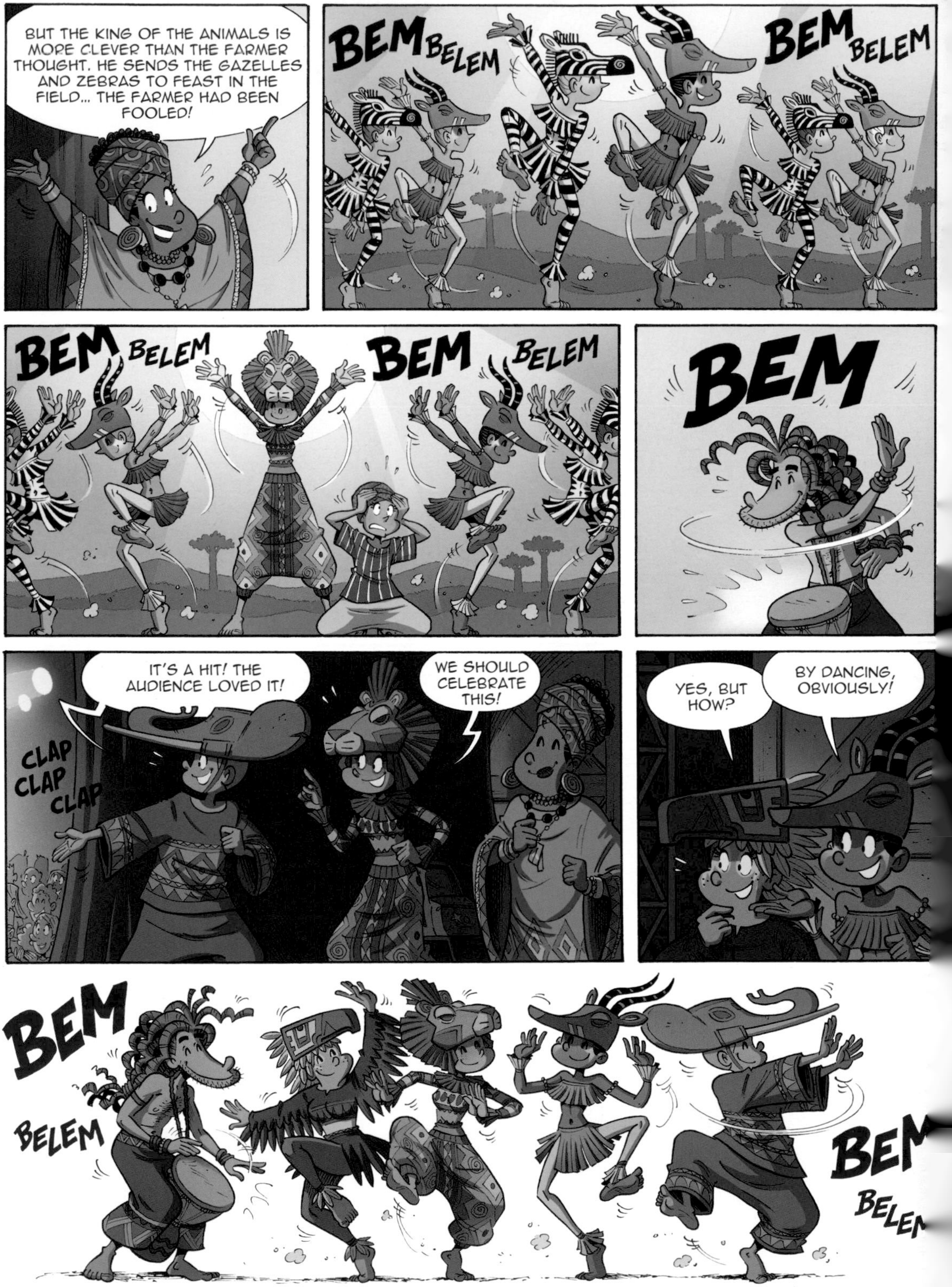
BUT THE KING OF THE ANIMALS IS MORE CLEVER THAN THE FARMER THOUGHT. HE SENDS THE GAZELLES AND ZEBRAS TO FEAST IN THE FIELD... THE FARMER HAD BEEN FOOLED!
BEM BELEM
BEM BELEM
BEM BELEM
BEM BELEM
BEM
CLAP CLAP CLAP
IT'S A HIT! THE AUDIENCE LOVED IT!
WE SHOULD CELEBRATE THIS!
YES, BUT HOW?
BY DANCING, OBVIOUSLY!
BEM
BELEM
BEM
BELEM

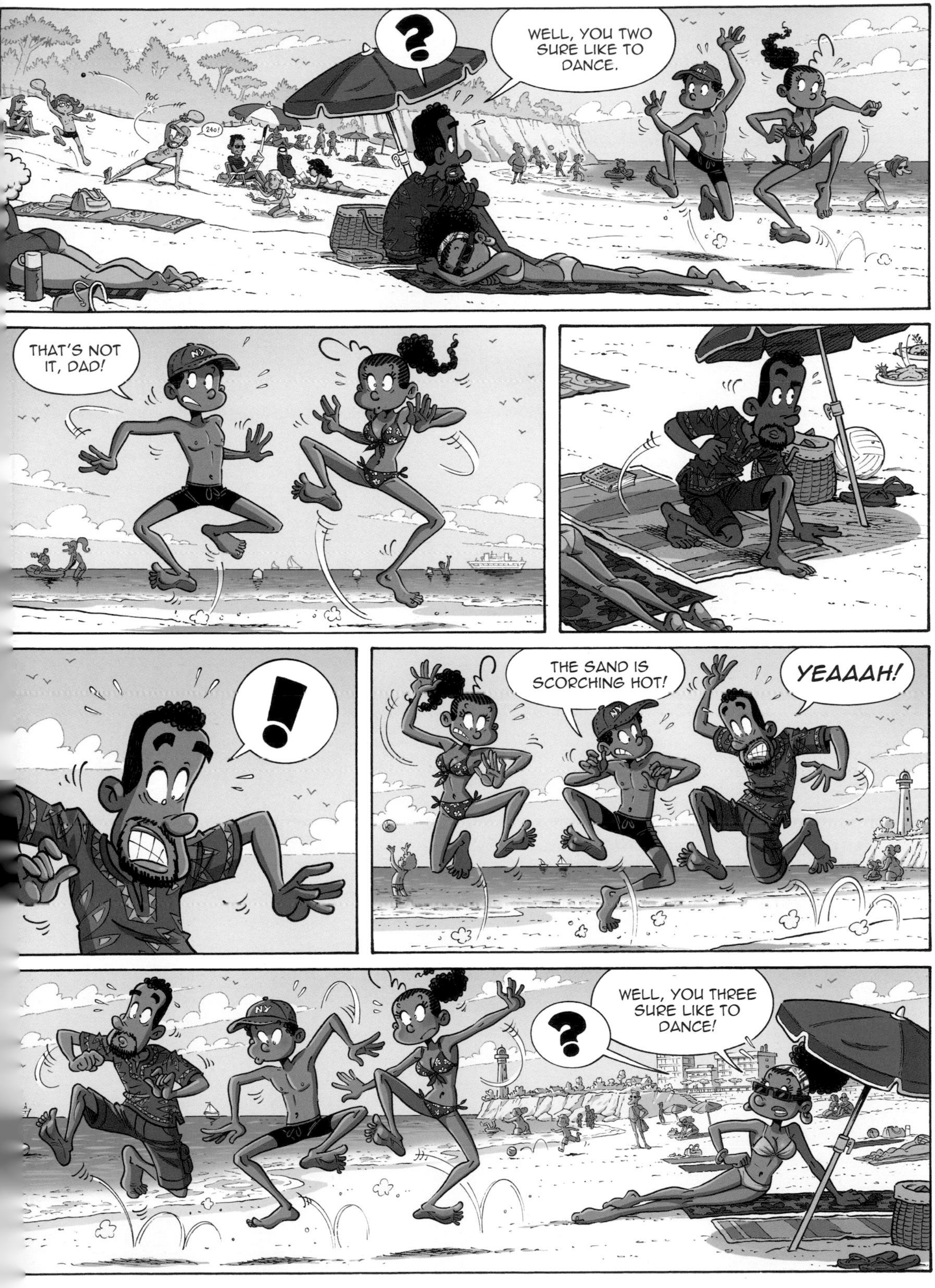
PoC
240!
?
WELL, YOU TWO SURE LIKE TO DANCE.
THAT'S NOT IT, DAD!
!
THE SAND IS SCORCHING HOT!
YEAAAH!
?
WELL, YOU THREE SURE LIKE TO DANCE!

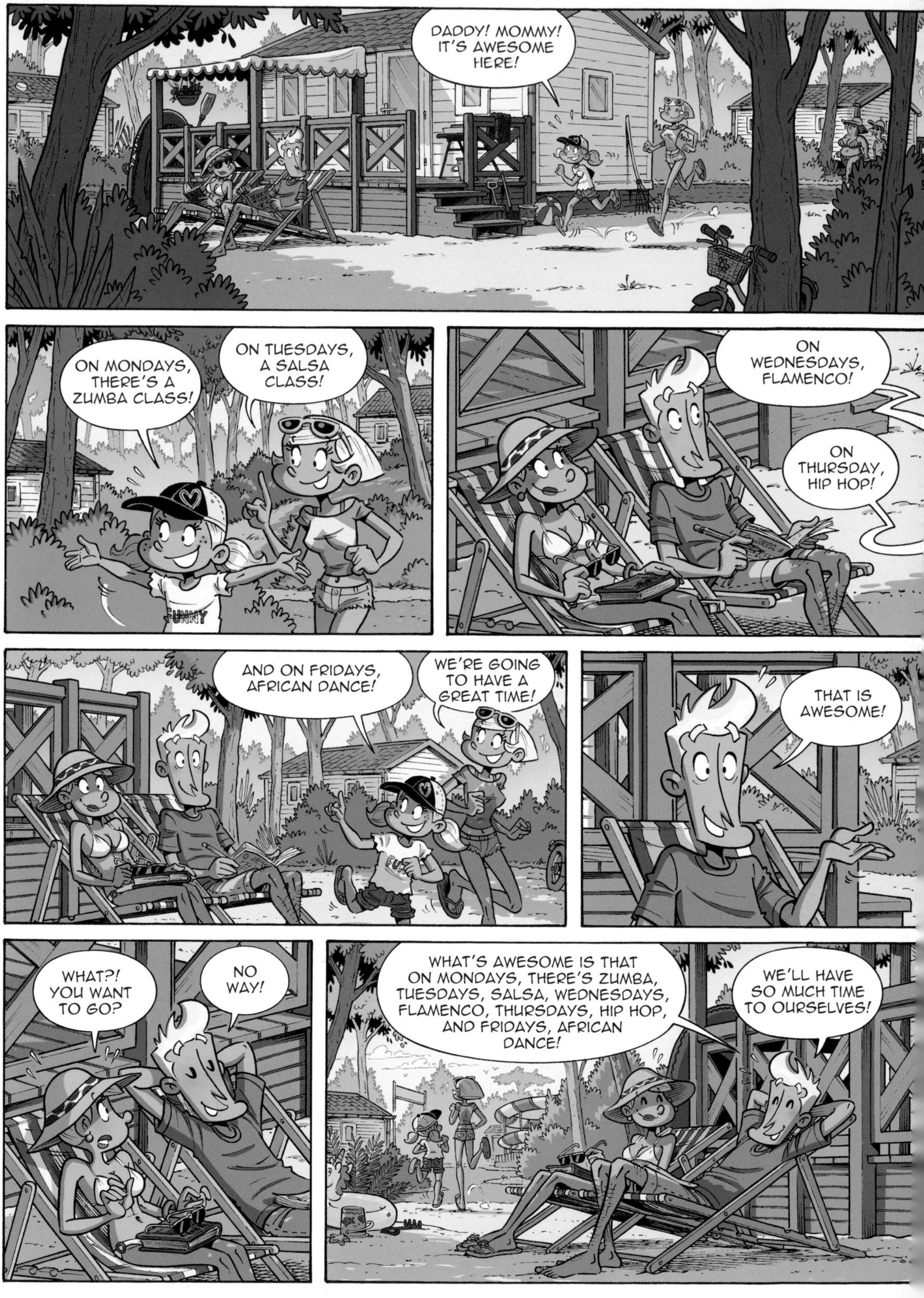
DADDY! MOMMY! IT'S AWESOME HERE!
ON MONDAYS, THERE'S A ZUMBA CLASS!
ON TUESDAYS, A SALSA CLASS!
ON WEDNESDAYS, FLAMENCO!
ON THURSDAY, HIP HOP!
AND ON FRIDAYS, AFRICAN DANCE!
WE'RE GOING TO HAVE A GREAT TIME!
THAT IS AWESOME!
WHAT?! YOU WANT TO GO?
NO WAY!
WHAT'S AWESOME IS THAT ON MONDAYS, THERE'S ZUMBA, TUESDAYS, SALSA, WEDNESDAYS, FLAMENCO, THURSDAYS, HIP HOP, AND FRIDAYS, AFRICAN DANCE!
WE'LL HAVE SO MUCH TIME TO OURSELVES!

WATCH OUT FOR PAPERCUTZ™

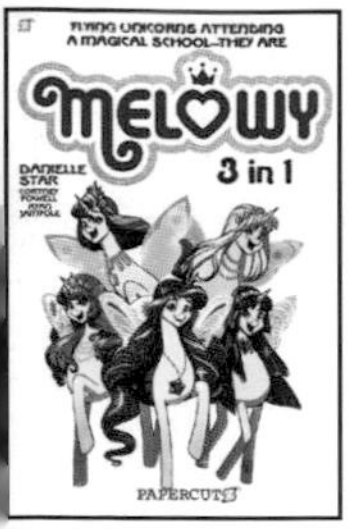

FLYING UNICORNS ATTENDING A MAGICAL SCHOOL—THEY ARE
MELOWY
3 in 1
PAPERCUTZ

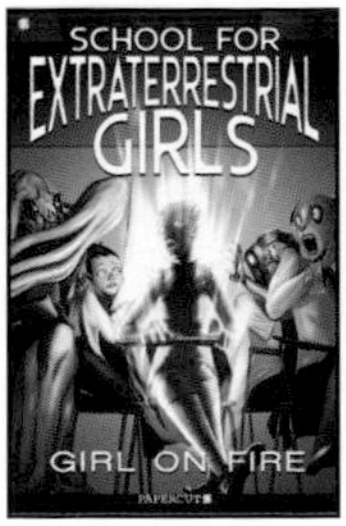

SCHOOL FOR EXTRATERRESTRIAL GIRLS
GIRL ON FIRE
PAPERCUTZ

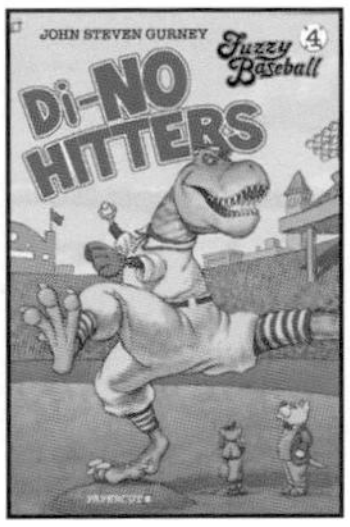

JOHN STEVEN GURNEY
Fuzzy Baseball
4
Di-NO HITTERS
PAPERCUTZ

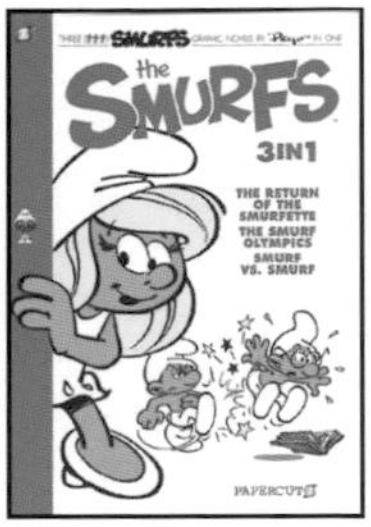

the SMURFS
3IN1
THE RETURN OF THE SMURFETTE
THE SMURF OLYMPICS
SMURF VS. SMURF
PAPERCUTZ

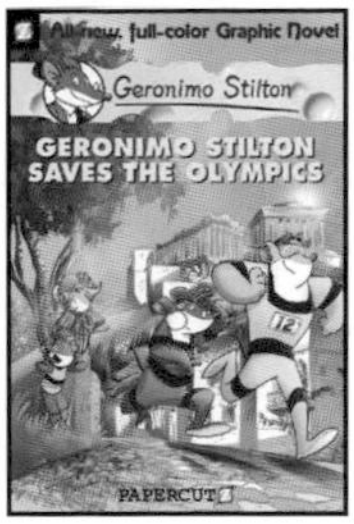

All-new, full-color Graphic Novel
Geronimo Stilton
GERONIMO STILTON SAVES THE OLYMPICS
PAPERCUTZ

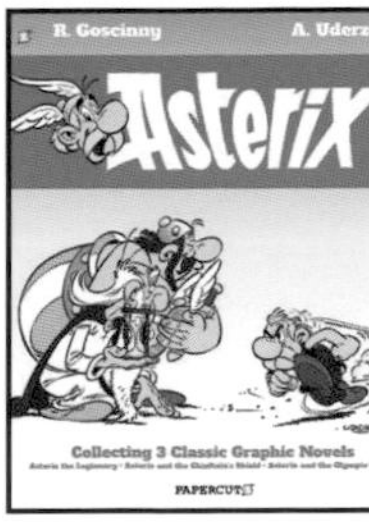

R. Goscinny
A. Uderzo
Asterix
Collecting 3 Classic Graphic Novels
PAPERCUTZ

Velcome to the classically-trained twelfth DANCE CLASS graphic novel by Crip & Béka, and Maëla Coson, from Papercutz, those day-dreaming wallflowers ledicated to publishing great graphic novels for all ages. I'm Jim Salicrup, the Editor-in-Chief and slow-dancing dude who dares to dance in public. Today ve're wondering if dancing and sports mix? And what etter way to decide the answer to any question than o look through a few Papercutz titles…

Vell, let's start with another girl named Maya, only this ne happens to be a Melowy, a flying unicorn. Maya, long with her fellow Melowies, Cleo, Cora, Selena, nd Electra attend a magical school called Destiny. It's little like DANCE CLASS, except instead of learning ow to dance, the Melowies are learning how to use neir special magical powers. Maya the Melowy and er friends compete against each other to make it nto their school team to ultimately compete against e male team from Chance, another magical school, the Aerobatic Tournament. While Melowy Maya oesn't make the team, one of her friends does— Cleo. nd one of the contests in the competition is interpre-ve dance! So, sports and dancing definitely mix in is magical world. There's even a celebratory dance hen the Tournament is over. If you're wondering hich team won, you'll have to pick up MELOWY 3 1 #1, by Cortney Powell, writer, and Ryan Jampole, tist, the answer will be found in "A Time to Fly."

the Papercutz graphic novel series SCHOOL FOR TRATERRESTRIAL GIRLS, by Jeremy Whitley, writer, d Jamie Noguchi, artist, we haven't yet seen if either orts or dance is on the curriculum, as the focus has en on Tara Smith, and how she becomes a student the top-secret school for female aliens. If that prem- sounds interesting to you, you should check this ies out. We suspect you'll enjoy meeting Tara and new friends, fellow students, and faculty.

ile sports is front and center in Papercutz graphic vel series FUZZY BASEBALL, by creator/writer/artist HN STEVEN GURNEY, we've yet to see any of the nwood Valley Fuzzies engage in a any dancing, not en a victory dance.

THE SMURFS, however, do sing and dance and play sports. Check out the various stories by creator/writer/artist Peyo collected in THE SMURFS 3 IN 1—you'll even find them competing in their own version of the Olympics. While the time-travelling GERONIMO STILTON has reluctantly competed in the Olympics (See GERONIMO STILTON #10 "Geronimo Stilton Saves the Olympics"), he hasn't been seen dancing yet. ASTERIX has also competed in the Olympics (See ASTERIX #4, by series creators René Goscinny, writer, and Albert Uderzo, artist, which includes "Asterix and the Olympic Games") and while we may not have seen Asterix himself dance, we certainly saw his best friend, Obelix, dance when in Spain (See ASTERIX #5 which features "Asterix in Spain").

We could go on and on through even more Papercutz series, but it seems like we've gotten the answer already. Sports and dance are not mutually exclusive. Some may be more passionate about one than the other, but it's fun to keep an open mind and be willing to give either a fair chance. You may discover a healthy new pastime. If nothing else it'll give you something fun to do while you're waiting for the next volume of DANCE CLASS.

Thanks, Jim

STAY IN TOUCH!

EMAIL:	salicrup@papercutz.com
WEB:	www.papercutz.com
INSTAGRAM:	@papercutzgn
TWITTER:	@papercutzgn
FACEBOOK:	PAPERCUTZGRAPHICNOVELS
FANMAIL:	Papercutz, 160 Broadway, Suite 700, East Wing, New York, NY 10038

Go to papercutz.com and sign up for the free Papercutz e-newsletter!

MORE GREAT GRAPHIC NOVEL SERIES AVAILABLE FROM

PAPERCUTZ™

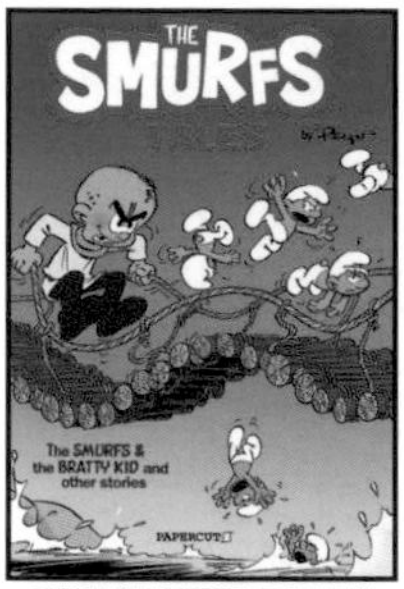
THE SMURFS
PAPERCUTZ

THE SMURF TALES

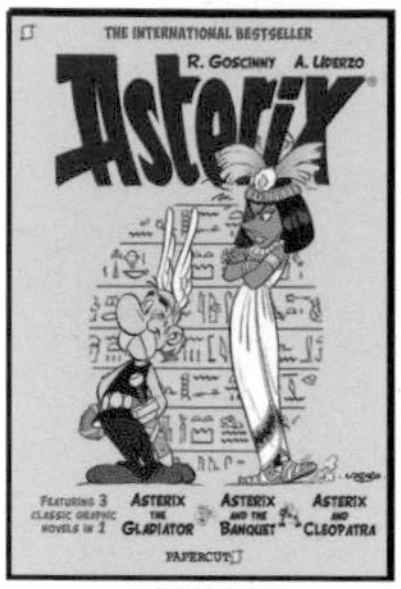
THE INTERNATIONAL BESTSELLER
R. GOSCINNY A. UDERZO
Asterix
PAPERCUTZ

ASTERIX

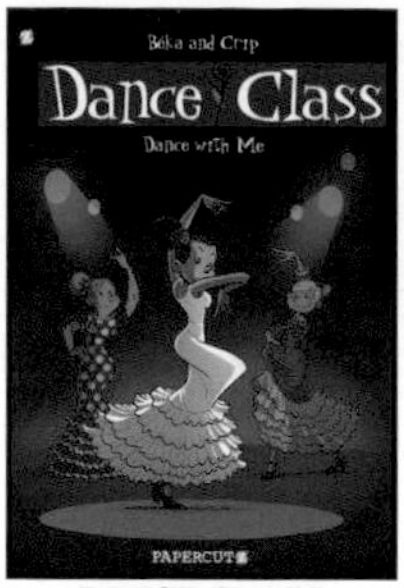
Béka and Crip
Dance Class
Dance with Me
PAPERCUTZ

DANCE CLASS

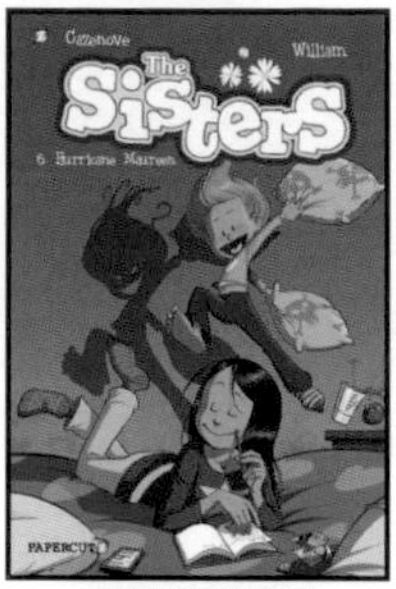
The Sisters
PAPERCUTZ

THE SISTERS

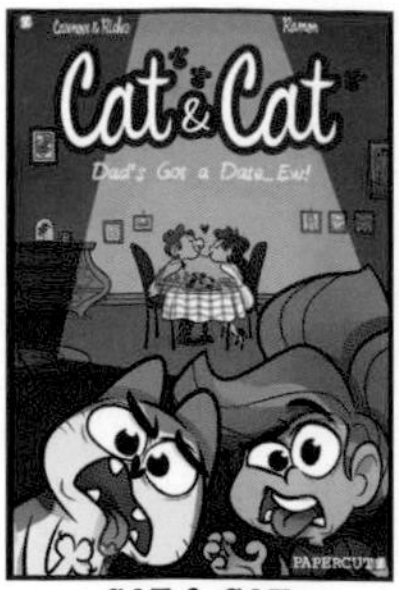
Cat & Cat
PAPERCUTZ

CAT & CAT

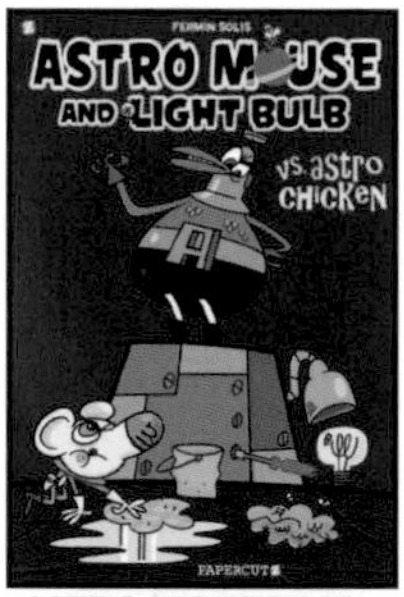
FERMIN SOLIS
ASTRO MOUSE AND LIGHT BULB
vs. astro CHICKEN
PAPERCUTZ

ASTRO MOUSE AND LIGHT BULB

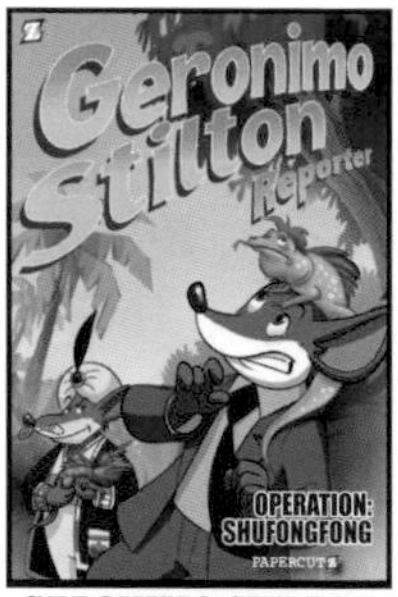
Geronimo Stilton Reporter
OPERATION: SHUFONGFONG
PAPERCUTZ

GERONIMO STILTON REPORTER

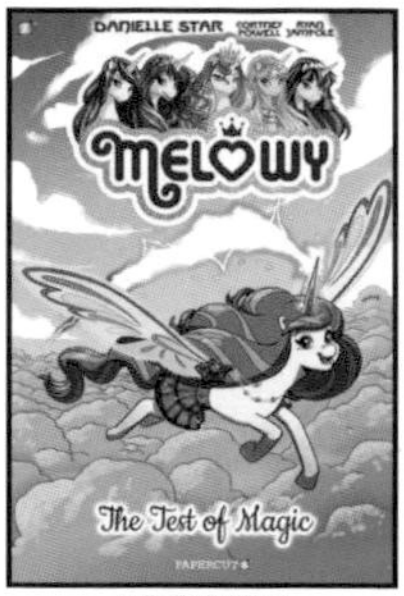
DANIELLE STAR
MELOWY
The Test of Magic
PAPERCUTZ

MELOWY

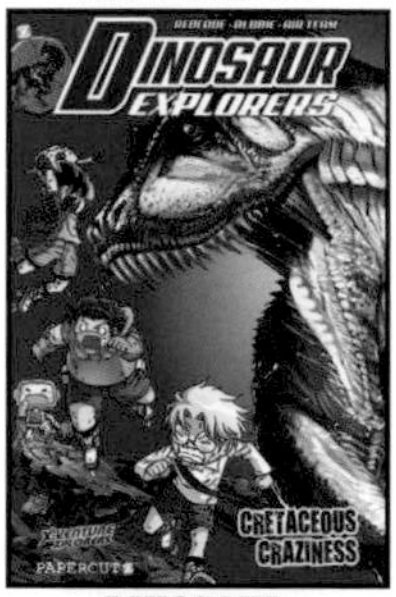
DINOSAUR EXPLORERS
CRETACEOUS CRAZINESS
PAPERCUTZ

DINOSAUR EXPLORERS

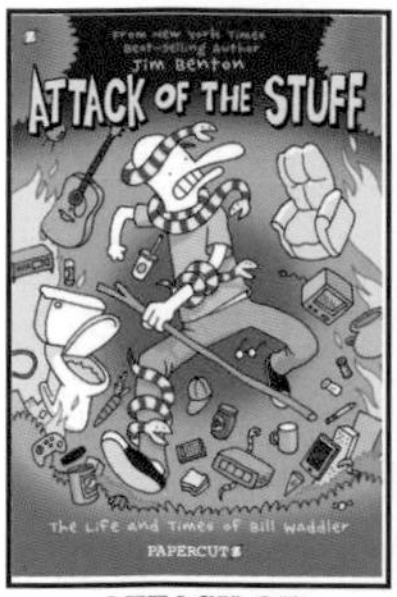
Jim Benton
ATTACK OF THE STUFF
PAPERCUTZ

ATTACK OF THE STUFF

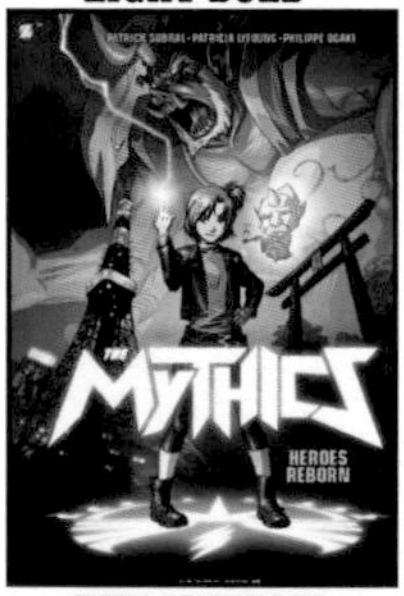
THE MYTHICS
HEROES REBORN

THE MYTHICS

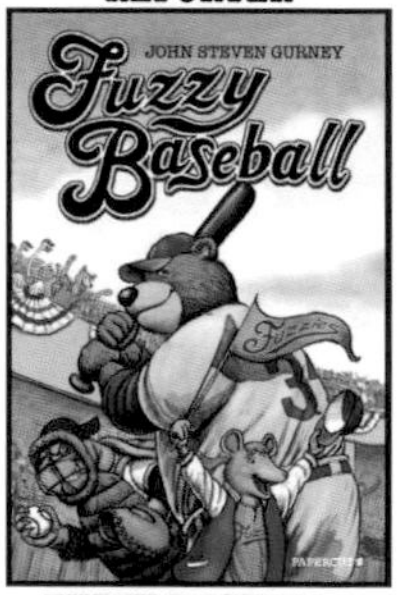
JOHN STEVEN GURNEY
Fuzzy Baseball
PAPERCUTZ

FUZZY BASEBALL

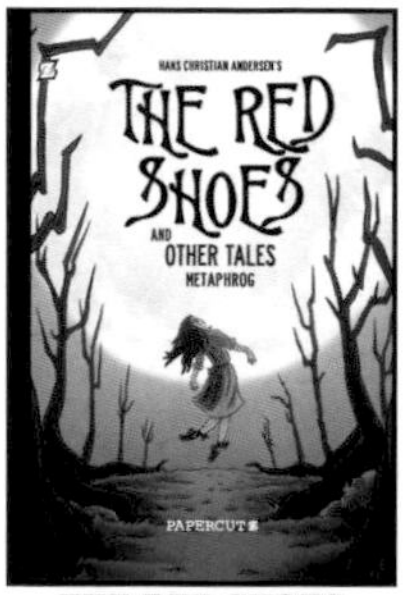
HANS CHRISTIAN ANDERSEN'S
THE RED SHOES
AND
OTHER TALES
METAPHROG
PAPERCUTZ

THE RED SHOES

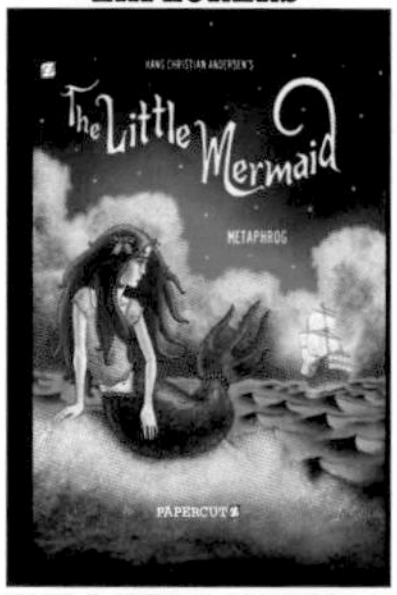
HANS CHRISTIAN ANDERSEN'S
The Little Mermaid
METAPHROG
PAPERCUTZ

THE LITTLE MERMAID

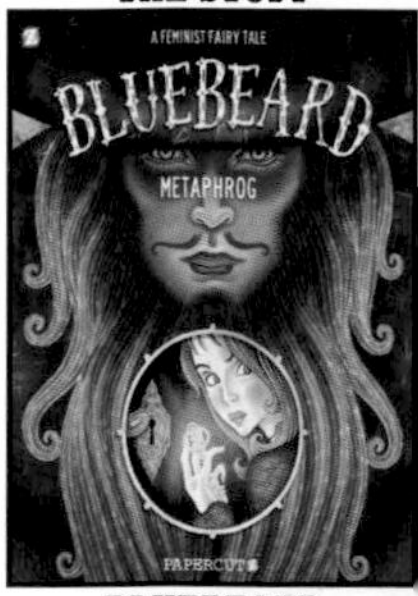
A FEMINIST FAIRY TALE
BLUEBEARD
METAPHROG
PAPERCUTZ

BLUEBEARD

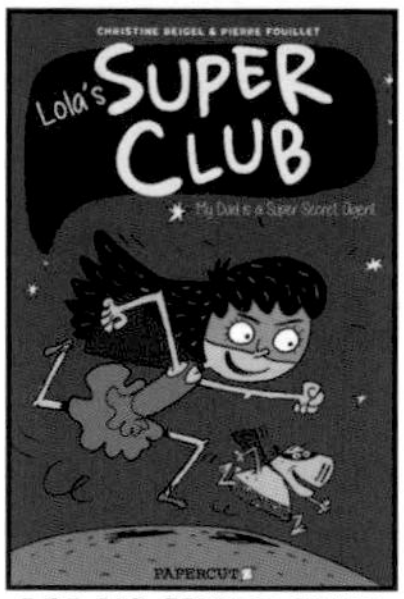
CHRISTINE BEIGEL & PIERRE FOUILLET
Lola's SUPER CLUB
PAPERCUTZ

LOLA'S SUPER CLUB

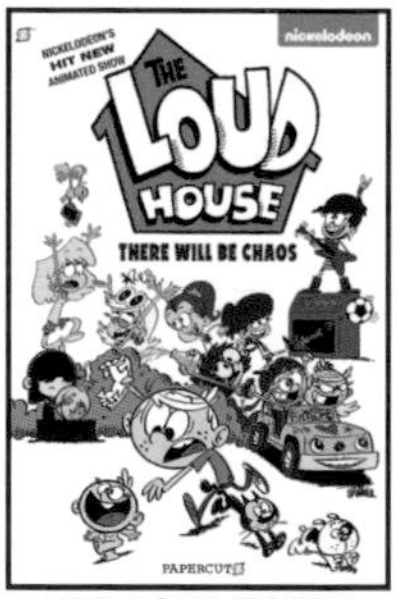
nickelodeon
THE LOUD HOUSE
THERE WILL BE CHAOS
PAPERCUTZ

THE LOUD HOUSE

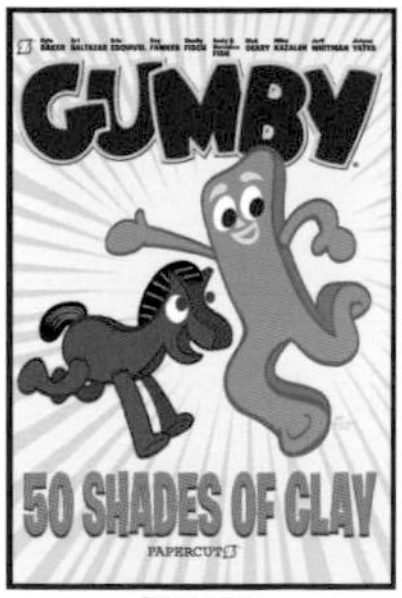
GUMBY
50 SHADES OF CLAY
PAPERCUTZ

GUMBY

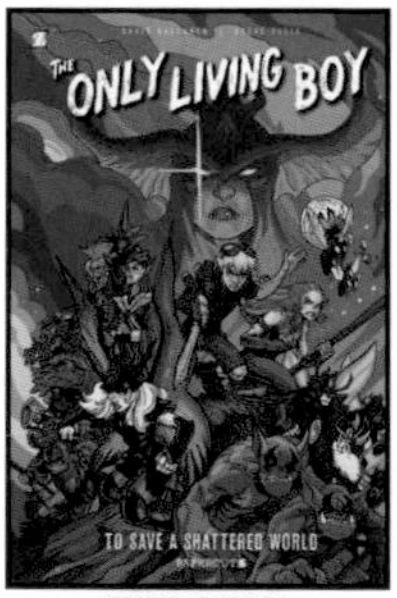
THE ONLY LIVING BOY
TO SAVE A SHATTERED WORLD

THE ONLY LIVING BOY

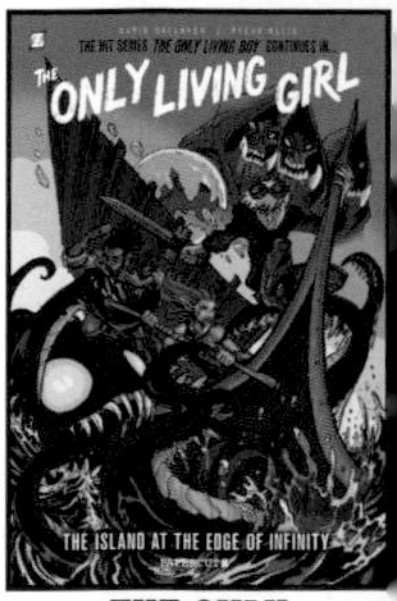
THE ONLY LIVING GIRL
THE ISLAND AT THE EDGE OF INFINITY

THE ONLY LIVING GIRL

Go to papercutz.com for more information

Also available where ebooks are sold.

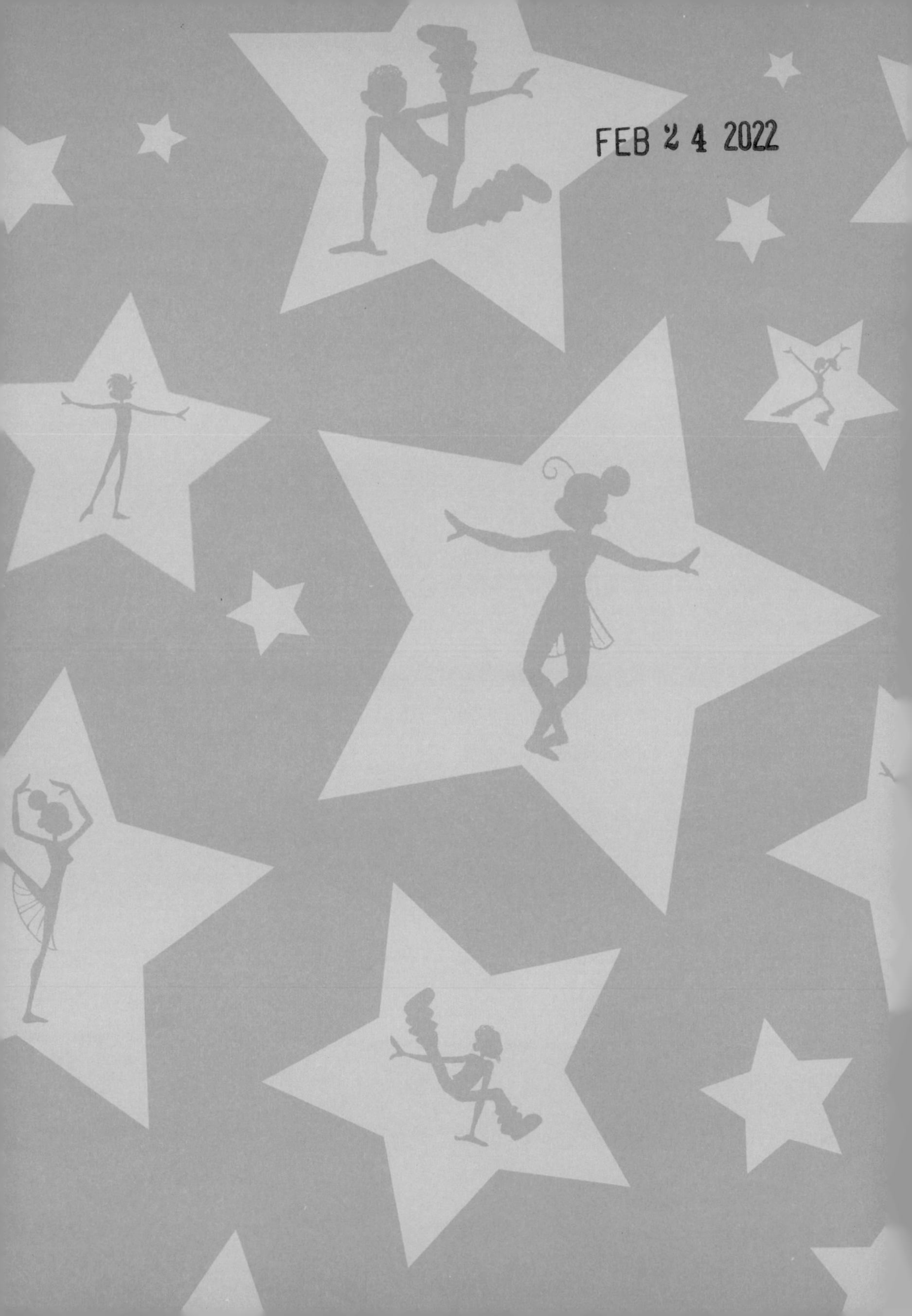